Sunday Golf

Lorraine M. Harris

PublishAmerica
Baltimore

© 2005 by Lorraine M. Harris.
All rights reserved. No part of this book may be reproduced, stored in a retrieval system or transmitted in any form or by any means without the prior written permission of the publishers, except by a reviewer who may quote brief passages in a review to be printed in a newspaper, magazine or journal.

First printing

At the specific preference of the author, PublishAmerica allowed this work to remain exactly as the author intended, verbatim, without editorial input.

ISBN: 1-4241-0252-9
PUBLISHED BY PUBLISHAMERICA, LLLP
www.publishamerica.com
Baltimore

Printed in the United States of America

To my husband, Lamont and our two daughters, Nicole and Natalie who always believed in me. As a novice golfer, I want to thank Lamont for being a patient, persistent, and loving Golf Coach to me, as well as to others, especially to Marlene and Edward (Big Guy) Collins.

CHAPTER 1

Mandy waited. It was just a matter of seconds before the tears would be streaming down her face. Then she felt the constriction in the middle of her chest. The twinge was so severe that every time it happened, she thought for sure she was going to have a heart attack or worse. The anxiety she felt each time she had a rendezvous with her lover could not go on much longer. The torment was more than she could have ever predicted. Although it was hard to admit, she knew that the tears and pangs of aching were caused by nothing more than—a guilty conscience.

As usual, she had turned her back to Lenny. Quietly, she let her tears fall. She hoped he would not say anything and she would probably be right. Usually, he did not extend any type of comfort to her and he seldom asked her why she was crying. To be honest, she knew the tears made him uncomfortable and in all probability, he did not want to know why their lovemaking brought her to tears.

Adultery was always wrong, but yet the relationship she had started outside of her marriage somehow was satisfying. At that moment the only thing Mandy could think about was a song, but she could not remember who sang it or all the words. However, the part of the song she could remember described exactly how she felt. *"How could something so wrong, feel so right?"*

As much as Mandy tried not to think about her husband, she could not put him out of her mind. Mandy loved her husband with all her heart but yet something had driven her to the point where she was now—in an affair. This was the first time she had ever cheated on him.

Was it possible that she could care that much for two people? She did not know. What she did recognize was that she did not like the deception. Early on into the affair, she realized how difficult it was for her to lie. Not to mention how complicated it was remembering the lies from the truths. Not telling the truth made Mandy feel as though she was performing a balancing act, similar to a trapeze artist. Gingerly, she was going back and forth between two men and at any moment she knew she could go plummeting to the bottom. There would be no safety net to catch her. As a result, she was not sure how much longer she could continue living a lie.

The affair had started almost six months ago. Now that she looked back, it should never have happened. When she met Lenny, she was the one who flirted ruthlessly with him and then insisted that they have a drink. Making love was not a question of if—but when. In fact, she would have been disappointed if the two of them had not ended up in bed.

For the first time in six months, Lenny heard Mandy sobbing out loud. He always knew she cried after they made love but she always made every effort not to let him hear her cry or see the tears. Therefore, he did not have to acknowledge the tears or ask what was wrong.

But today for some reason Lenny questioned her. "What's wrong?"

Composing herself, Mandy used the back of her hand to wipe away the tears that were falling down her cheeks.

"I'm okay, it's nothing," she lied.

"I'm just having a blue day which is typical for a woman who's going through menopause." Lately, that was her excuse for everything—insomnia, being short-tempered, being irritable, and having an affair.

"Listen Mandy, we need to talk. Something has been on my mind and I need to tell you how I feel."

Lenny paused for a moment. Mandy could tell he was choosing his words too carefully. Hoping he would not say the "L" word, she closed her eyes briefly.

Quickly, she said a prayer. *"God, give me strength. I can't handle hearing him say he loves me."*

"I don't know where to begin," he said pausing.

"Please look at me." He waited until Mandy turned her body toward him.

"I fully understood what I was getting into when we started this relationship. You made it very clear that you were married and you would never leave your husband, but…"

Mandy did not give Lenny an opportunity to finish his sentence. In addition, she made no effort to hide the annoyance in her voice.

"But what?"

"Please let me explain. Somewhere during these six months, my feelings have changed. I have to be honest. I want more than just Tuesdays and Thursdays. I never thought I would say this but…" Lenny tried to conceal his frustration.

"I want, no I need more than just "bed" time." He let out a nervous laugh.

"I want us to be able to do normal things, like go out to dinner or to the movies. I would give anything if we could spend the night together and to have you wake up in my arms…"

"Please don't." She put her fingers to Lenny's mouth to silence him. Dropping her fingers, she turned away from him and got up. Hurriedly, she began putting her clothes on. There was tension and silence in the room that seemed to linger too long. It was similar to the cloud of smoke that stays in a room when people smoke.

Reaching out to Mandy, Lenny waited for her to act in response. She did not react. Her full attention was fastening the buttons on her blouse.

"I'm sorry if I upset you, but to be honest I don't know how much longer I can continue doing this. Having been married before, I should have realized that this would bother me more than I thought it would. Lately, I haven't been able to stop thinking about your husband and how he would feel if he knew his wife was with another man."

He waited for Mandy to say something, anything. Again, she did not respond. Her concentration was putting on her earrings.

"I know you don't want to hear this, but have you ever thought about leaving your husband?"

"You know that's impossible!" Shaking her head, she said quite emphatically.

"Not to mention, I wouldn't leave him anyway." In a second—fear, anger, and sadness crossed her face.

She continued in a soft, tender tone. "Look, we agreed from the beginning, that this could only be an affair. Nothing else, there would be no strings attached."

The tone of her voice changed from tenderness to anxiety. "Even if I wanted to leave my husband, there is no way that I would. Besides, if my husband found out about you and me, he'd kill both of us. Am I making myself clear?"

It dismayed her that she was having this conversation. As much as she would hate to end the affair, she would. The last thing she wanted was to hurt anyone, especially her husband. There was no way she was going to risk her marriage. In addition, she would do everything she could to protect her husband from finding out about her infidelity.

Mandy loved her husband. So what happened? She could not quite pin point when she and her husband started having marital problems. Thinking about it, she had not intended the affair to start at all. There were times when Mandy thought she was surely dreaming because in 17 years, she had never cheated on her husband. In fact, being with another man had never crossed her mind. Unexpectedly, it just happened.

Then she thought about her mother. No, the affair did not just happen. What was it her mother used to say? *"For every decision you make, there's always a consequence."*

Having no answers, Mandy thought about how she could easily see herself with Lenny if she was not married. However, that was not the case. She was very much married.

What had she been thinking about? How and why did she let what was supposed to be innocent flirting turn into a full, fledged affair?

CHAPTER 2

Thinking about the time when the affair started, Mandy could only think about how everything seemed to point to the day when her doctor told her she was menopausal. Somehow, menopause meant she would no longer have sex appeal—she no longer had a choice about having children. She could not help but think about her mother and her mother's sisters, her aunts—they represented menopause and they were old. Although Mandy had not discussed "menopause" with her mother and aunts she had heard them talking in whispers about their hot flashes, night sweats, vaginal dryness, and their forgetfulness.

Now, she was like them and she was part of that unspoken club—similar to the club all women join when they start having their menstrual period. She remembered her mother and aunts celebrating her big day. At the time, she saw nothing to rejoice about in having a monthly period. If she were to tell them that she was menopausal, she would shudder to think what they might want to do to celebrate her coming into a different phase of her life.

Their menopausal conversations seemed more about their physical changes. Her changes seemed some how different. For some reason, she felt a need that she could not explain. Not only had she watched her body go through physical changes but mentally she was not the same person. She seemed to want and need more, as a woman.

Her husband not wanting to understand menopause did not help her situation. He was old school. He did not want to hear about things like menopause. It was hard enough when she had a monthly period. When her husband was working, he used to schedule his business trips around or during the time when she was menstruating.

To make menopause an easier transition for them, she had scheduled several doctor appointments for her and her husband to discuss the subject. Every appointment she made for them, he called and canceled or never showed up. To quote him he said, *"Menopause was a woman's problem, not his."*

Her husband liked it better when women did not talk about women issues openly. It was his preference that women topics be discussed in "hushed" tones among women. It bothered Mandy deeply that her husband did not care enough to want to understand how menopause was affecting her, as well as him and their marriage.

Mandy knew that menopause had not been easy for her husband. The hardest change for her husband had been her mood swings. Mandy knew that there were times when she would be smiling and happy one minute and then she acted like a raving lunatic. The hot flashes were uncontrollable, one minute she seemed normal and then water was dripping off her face as if someone had poured it over her head. The night sweats required them to get up and change the bed because it was as if she had urinated.

Mandy knew her husband tried to be patient. At times he was even sympathetic, but other times, it was just too overwhelming for him. Then he would pester her and ask continuously. *"What do other women do? Can't your doctor give you some kind of medicine or something to help you?"*

Explaining to her husband that she could not take hormone replacement therapy—HRT—was useless. At one point, she did take HRT and it really helped to ease her symptoms. However, because her mother and her aunts had experienced the threat of breast cancer, she was terrified. Explaining her family medical history to her doctor, Mandy was told that she was in a high-risk category for possibly getting breast cancer. Without hesitation, she took the doctor's advice and stopped taking HRT.

There were times when her husband said that she acted as if menopause was life threatening, similar to cancer. He wanted and suggested to her to take HRT anyway. As he put it, *"We all have to die from something."*

To help her husband understand the reasons why she did not—no should not take HRT, she researched the Internet for articles on the subject. She printed out the most recent medical journal articles that supported the fact that menopausal women should not be taking HRT because of the potentially harmful side effects. But those articles were not convincing enough for her husband. As a result, menopause had become a "do not" discuss subject between the two of them.

Whom was she fooling? She could not put all the blame on her husband or on menopause. There were other contributing factors that caused her to have an affair. One big factor that was constantly on her mind and she was having a difficult time coping with was the changes she had been observing in her aging husband. When Mandy looked at him, she was beginning to see visions of an old man, similar to her father.

For some reason her husband who was almost twenty years older than her, no longer looked vibrant and young. She felt and visibly saw the signs of him growing old. Where his hair had been black and gray at the temples, it was now almost all white. Where once his embrace was physically powerful and muscular, his arms now felt weak and frail.

From the beginning when she started dating her husband, her friends and family warned her about marrying an older man. Refusing to listen to them, she married him anyway. At the beginning of their marriage, they were like any other newly wed couple. She could not have been a happier woman.

It was not until her husband retired from his job that she really began to notice the age difference and it just wasn't about sex. He had begun to slow down. Mandy found herself alone most nights because by eight o'clock her husband wanted or needed to go to bed. She found he had lost his aspiration and desire to do anything.

"Earth to Mandy." Lenny had been trying to get Mandy's attention.

He tried again. "Hello, Mandy." She finally looked up.

"I've been talking to you but you seemed lost in your thoughts. What's going on?"

"I'm sorry, I was just thinking about my..." She didn't finish the sentence as she reminded herself that discussing her husband with Lenny was off limits. From the start of the affair, she had made a pact with herself not to talk to Lenny about her husband and she was not about to start now.

"Nothing's wrong," she said hastily.

"Listen, I got to go." Mandy scanned the room, making sure she had not left anything.

"My husband has been watching me like a teenager with a curfew. If I'm one minute late, he drills me as if he's conducting an interrogation, wanting a detailed account of my whereabouts. As much as possible, I tell him the truth. Therefore, I don't have to worry about getting caught in a lie." Mandy saw the hurt look in her lover's eyes but she did not want to be late.

"Listen. I'm really sorry. I wish I could stay longer, but..." She stopped in mid-sentence. There was no need in continuing this line of discussion. She had to leave.

"I promise I'll make it up to you another time." Weakly, she gave him a smile.

They embraced. She willed herself not to cry. Tenderly, he kissed her.

Releasing her, he whispered, "I wish you didn't have to go, but I understand. Will I see you Thursday?"

"I'm not sure, I'll call you."

Deeply, they kissed again. Tightly, Lenny held her. He didn't want to let her go. Feeling Mandy pulling away gently, he finally freed her from his embrace. She looked at him, turned and he watched her walk out the door.

CHAPTER 3

Amanda yelled, "Woody."
"I'm coming."
"I'm sorry about yelling, but you're going to be late for your golf lesson."
"So what if I am? It's not like this is something I wanted to do. Remember, this was your idea, not mine."
"You need to quit pouting like a little boy who is being made to do something he doesn't want to do. I want you to take these lessons so you'll have something constructive to do with your time." Amanda looked at Woody as he continued to sulk.
"Besides, why live in Florida if you don't know how to golf?"
"The weather," he responded sarcastically.
"Yeah, whatever." Amanda didn't want this conversation to be a tit for tat, but she did want to make her point.
"Listen Woody, I want you to remember, these golf lessons aren't just about you. I enjoy golfing and it would be nice if you could golf with me. Before I retire, we need to start developing some common interests. To start, I thought that if you learned how to golf that would be one interest we'd have in common. We need to be able to do things apart as well as together."

"Whatever!"

"Look Woody. Retirement is not a death sentence. I want our retirement to be fun, enjoyable, you know...active. When I retire, I plan on golfing..." Before Amanda could finish her sentence, her husband interrupted her.

"Good for you, you have my permission to golf as often as you like."

There was a harshness in Woody's voice and he knew it. He was growing tired of his wife insisting that he needed to be doing things other than sleeping, reading books, or watching television game shows.

Amanda started to say something and then she stopped. They looked at each other but neither one of them said anything. Amanda was brooding as she pondered over what to say next.

Woody sighed in frustration. He thought about how he was quite content with his retirement life. For the first time in his adult life, he could do what he wanted and when he wanted. He had no one to answer to and he had no place pressing to go. He was happy doing nothing.

To be honest, Woody felt as though he had accomplished everything professionally, as well as socially that he cared to do. He had retired as a CEO, traveled throughout the United States and some foreign countries, raised a family, and had been an avid tennis player and bowler.

Thinking about it, Woody knew he wasn't being fair to Amanda. He understood that she wanted to do some of the things he had already done, but he had little or no desire to repeat some of those activities.

Woody recognized that their problem was deeper than just *"doing things together."* Regardless of how he and Amanda ignored the subject, some of their disagreements had to do with their age difference. Unfortunately, he had no idea how to resolve that conflict. After all, there was no magic formula in making him younger. It's not like they could turn back the clock of time. He guessed he was going to have to compromise and accept the fact that his retirement was not just about him.

Constantly, he had to remind himself that he had married a younger woman. She was still young and energetic. Intellectually, Woody understood Amanda's requests for him to be more active, it's just that he didn't want to. However, he knew he had to make some changes as he recalled some words a man once told him. *"You must use it or lose it."*

"Look Amanda, my Manda Bear." Usually once he used his pet name for her, she would smile and forget why she was upset with him. But not today, she stood stoned face, no smile to be seen.

Softening his tone Woody continued. "Listen sweetheart, I can see how important retirement is to you. Unfortunately, I'm just now beginning to understand how much our ideas about retirement are different. So just for you, I'll learn how to golf."

Stretching his arms out to grab his wife Woody teased. "Instead of me taking golfing lessons today, I can think of something else we might want to do."

Playfully, she dodged his out reached hands and smiled with a response. "We could but it's getting late, you better get going."

Hesitating for a moment, Amanda said, "Oh by the way, I thought that while you're taking your lesson, I would go to Mass."

"I don't think so darling."

Authoritatively, Woody said, "When I return from my golf lesson, we'll have plenty of time to go to the one o'clock Mass."

"Fine. Whatever." Under her breath, Amanda had let her words slip out. She hoped Woody had not heard her. Unfortunately, he had.

Quickly, he asked, "What does that mean?"

"Nothing Woody." Amanda spoke through gritted teeth as she let out a heavy sigh.

If she had told him what she really thought, it would have started an argument that she did not want to have. Their morning had been stressful enough. In addition, her head was beginning to pound and she did not want it to turn into a full-fledged headache.

"You're going to be late for your lesson if you don't hurry."

Woody wrapped Amanda in his arms and held her tightly. Looking at her with tender eyes, Woody kissed her good-bye.

CHAPTER 4

Pacing the floor, Bob Webster looked at his watch. It was getting late. He wondered why his wife had asked him to wait for her? If she did not hurry, he was going to be late for his golf lesson.

He yelled, "Vanessa, I need to go. Hurry up."

"Just give me a few more minutes." Vanessa was hurrying as fast as she could. It was a last minute idea to go to the golf range with him. She hoped that he was not losing his patience, which would turn into him getting angry with her.

Bob was trying very hard not to let his temper get the best of him. Being married just a little over a year he knew he had to show a certain amount of patience. However, she was beginning to test his tolerance when it came to her wants and needs.

When they got married, he never envisioned spending every waking moment with her. Bob tried explaining to his lovely wife that they should have separate interests, friends, and hobbies. So far, she had not accepted, understood, or embraced the idea. When he brought the subject up for discussion, either they ended up arguing or she went into a quiet stupor and refused to talk to him about it.

Bob wasn't sure why Nessa, the pet name he had given her, had become so insecure. When they were dating, she had enough confidence for both of them. She knew who she was and what she wanted. But since they had gotten married, she had changed. He wondered what was really bothering her?

Surely, Nessa could not be concerned about their age difference. For a woman of 38, Nessa was in fantastic physical condition. Her body was a perfect 36-26-38 which caused men and women to gaze at her. Her brown skin was as smooth as silk with little or no visible signs of aging. Her shoulder length, dark brown hair was accented with deep dark brown eyes. She was an amazing, beautiful woman. He was 30 and most people, including his family, thought she was younger than him.

As far as Bob was concerned, the difference in their age was not a factor. He never gave it a second thought. However, if he was honest about it before they got married, Nessa did express occasional doubts about her being almost ten years older than him. He was the one who always dismissed her misgivings.

Well, they were married until death do they part. Age was merely a number and it was not important to him. He had almost given up the idea of finding a woman to love and to marry. All the women he had dated before he met Nessa had been a walking advertisement for reasons why a man did not want to get married—too possessive, less than truthful, and too money-oriented. Bob would have to do more to assure his stunning wife that he could care less about her being older than him.

Frustration laced his voice as he said, "Nessa, hurry up."

"Why do you want me to wait for you?" I need to go or I'm going to be late for my first golf lesson."

"I thought I'd go along with you." She tried to read his reaction. She couldn't so she rushed on.

"While you're taking your lesson, I thought I'd hit some balls on the practice golf range. After your lesson, we could go to breakfast or brunch or something?"

"Why don't I take my first golf lesson, then maybe next Sunday, you could tag along?" The tone of his voice came across more unyielding than he intended it to be.

Turning her head, Vanessa made an attempt to cover up the fact that tears had started to well up in her eyes. Inhaling deeply and exhaling, Bob made every effort to hide his irritation.

Walking over to his wife, Bob put his arms around her, and embraced her tightly. He wanted her to feel his love. He smoothed her hair and rocked her soothingly.

Then in her ear, he whispered in a soft, comforting tone. "Sweetie, I love you. It's not that I don't want you going with me."

He eased his embrace. He wanted to look into her eyes when he spoke.

He continued speaking in a gentle tone. "This is something I have to do alone."

Pulling away from her, he kissed the top of her forehead before continuing. "Remember, you're the one who suggested I take these golf lessons."

Tenderly, he reminded her, "You're the one who thought that if I learned to golf that it might be beneficial to our real estate business."

Although Bob asked the question, he didn't want an answer. "Do you remember?"

Continuing, he said, "You already golf. As you well know, I don't know the first thing about golf. As a result, I don't want you watching me make mistakes while I'm trying to learn. You know how I can be with my fragile male ego." He slid his hands down to Nessa's behind.

He added, "besides, I want to be able to beat your cute little butt when I do learn how to golf." He caressed her behind and gave her a playful smack. Vanessa wiggled, letting out a small giggle.

"I'm sorry. I just thought that with this being Sunday and the last day of our weekend that we might be able to spend it together."

Looking into her eyes, he thought he detected tears. He hoped that she was not going to start crying.

Sweetly, he said, "I understand what you're saying and I'm not dismissing you. I want to spend Sundays with you too, but until these lessons are over, our Sunday mornings will be a little different. We won't be able to spend them together. But when I return from my lesson, I'm all yours and we can do whatever you want." He put his hand under her chin and titled it upward.

"Now give me a big smile."

Faintly, Vanessa smiled. They kissed and Bob hurried out the door.

CHAPTER 5

"Donnie, what time is your golf lesson over?"
He stopped for a minute before answering. "I'm not sure."
"The golf lesson begins at eight o'clock and it should probably end at nine o'clock. After the official lesson, I'm not sure what else is required. Why, what's up?"
"I just thought I might meet you at the golf range. Then maybe we could go to brunch or something?"
Donnie hoped that his answer would not cause an argument. At times Raymond could make Donnie feel terrible about not boasting to the world that he was gay. In the case of his golf lessons, he would prefer that the men not know his sex preference and it had nothing to do with him being ashamed of his sexuality.
It was just like at work, Raymond wanted him to tell his co-workers that he was gay. Donnie saw no purpose in doing so. Most of his co-workers did not know about his sexual orientation. The few that knew it did not appear to care. It wasn't that he was hiding his "gayness" but he did not want to be ostracized by his colleagues.
He had already experienced discrimination in the work place as a black man so why add the possibility of further prejudice by telling

his co-workers that he was gay? In his career field as an investment banker he had successfully advanced to an executive position, but not without having to walk on water and part the Red Sea. Currently, he felt as though he was making strives in improving the advancement for minorities. He had earned his co-workers respect on his own merits. So why should he rock the boat?

Raymond was patting his foot and he had crossed his arms across his chest. He was waiting impatiently for an answer.

Before Donnie answered Raymond, he took a deep inward breath and exhaled. He knew Raymond would be less than pleased with his reply.

"I don't think meeting me at the golf range is such a good idea."

"What do you mean Donnie Wilson?" Raymond's voice reached a high pitch that indicated to Donnie that he could be in for an argument.

Exhaling, Raymond rolled his eyes in disgust at Donnie. Raymond didn't want to quarrel with him over this issue. However, it infuriated him when Donnie played both sides of the fence—being straight and gay to suit the situation. Raymond knew that Donnie had a tendency to do what made him feel comfortable. It was like Donnie was out of the closet but in the closet too.

Slowly Raymond said. "I know that look Donnie. We have been together for three years. I would have thought by now it wouldn't bother you to have people see us together as a couple."

"Look, that's not it and you know it. It's just that these guys are probably all straight. I don't want to begin my golf lessons with them knowing that I'm gay."

Donnie stopped and looked at Raymond. At least, Donnie wanted Raymond to acknowledge that he understood but instead Donnie was looking at an irritated facial expression.

"I want them to get to know me first—as a man—not as a "gay" man."

"Oh please." With a horror-struck look and his tone laced with bitterness, Raymond chastised him.

"Who gives a hoot about these men?" Raymond did not let

Donnie continue as he pressed on.

"Besides, what do you care about these men?" Donnie started to respond but Raymond went on with another question.

"And while we're talking about it, just how often do you deny being gay?"

Raymond was on a roll and he was not giving Donnie an opportunity to defend himself.

"I mean what difference does it make if these men know you're gay?"

Donnie and Raymond locked eyes as if they were getting ready to do battle. Donnie didn't respond immediately. He was waiting to see if Raymond had calmed down or whether he was going to ask another round of pointless questions.

Finally, in a stern reply, Donnie said, "Raymond, I'm not sure why you went there. I mean I'll admit that there are times when I have used the "Don't ask, don't tell," Clinton Administration's policy."

Donnie looked at Raymond who didn't say anything. Donnie had turned the tables on him.

"Besides, don't tell me you haven't used the policy."

Looking shyly, Raymond did not answer him right away. He was self employed and owned an investigative and security company. As a result, there were certain clients where he had to pretend to be straight when doing business with them. If he had not, it could have cost him money.

"I hate to admit it, but you're right. I detest not being who I am. However, even in today's climate of acceptance, everyone isn't ready for homosexuals and I know that. Not to mention how prejudice people can be, especially men. Yeah, I feel ya. I'm not mad at you. I don't like it and I do understand. I'm sorry. You do what you have to do."

"I'll call you when the lesson is over. I can meet you somewhere or you can wait until I come home."

"How about meeting me at Applebee's on Route 27/441."

"That'll work." They kissed and Donnie left.

CHAPTER 6

Sundays had become quiet, uneventful, boring days. However, Lenny Harper had been looking forward to this particular Sunday. With his recent divorce, the house had an overpowering quietness. He didn't miss his third wife, but he missed her presence. For some reason, when it was just Lenny in the house, it just did not feel lived in—there was an unexplained void.

In all reality, he liked being married but so far he had not been able to pick the right woman. As he thought about the women he had married he wondered how he had made so many bad choices.

His first wife, Kimberly, was cute as a button but she was strictly about being intellectual. She had little or no common sense. She spent money like she had a money press and could print money, as she needed it. In addition, she did not like to work. After they got married and without any discussion with him, she announced she had quit her job. She had decided to get yet another master's degree. Lenny agreed she could get another degree but he was not willing to pay for it. After all, how many master degrees did she need? So, she left him.

Wife number two was Christine. She was nice, loving, and could cook like his grandmother—everything from scratch. She could have started her own restaurant with her family's fried chicken and cornbread recipes. After they got married, Christine told Lenny that she required a certain amount of time where she could reflect and meditate. Lenny's house had three bedrooms, a den, and a home office. Lenny understood the fact that she needed her own space and told her to pick a room that she might want to fix up as her own. Methodically, she explained to Lenny that she needed more than just her own private room. Therefore, she would be keeping her condo, which would serve as a place of solace when she needed time alone.

At first, Lenny thought he could deal with her needing time by herself but eventually Christine was spending more time at her condo than with him. He never knew what she did when she spent time by herself. When he asked, she replied nicely but firmly that it was basically none of his business. She could not understand why he did not comprehend her need to have time alone. When he could no longer tolerate all the solo time she required, he ended the marriage.

Lastly, there was Shirley. When he thought about Shirley, he always had a sense of sadness because he truly thought Shirley was going to be his true and lasting love. No such luck. Keeping secrets and telling lies were Shirley's specialty. When he reminisced about it, he should have been suspicious about the fact that he had never met a single person in her family, nor any of her friends.

After they got married, it became clear why he had not met her relatives and friends. She had been keeping a secret that she could not afford to reveal. Shirley waited three months and then gave him the biggest surprise of his life—she told him that she had five children. She explained that she did not tell him about the children before they got married because she was afraid that he could not accept her and the children. At first, Lenny thought Shirley was joking about the children. Then he met them. He suspected that she was more afraid that he could not accept her five children because they looked as though each one had a different Father but Lenny never asked. Despite how much Lenny tried to make their marriage work, he had a difficult time forgiving Shirley for her trickery, less than truthfulness, and the lies. The trust was beyond repair.

Perhaps he could have accepted the children but he had wanted an opportunity to know about them before he had married her. He had felt betrayed. The whole year they dated, she never once mentioned she had children. Before they got married, they had even received marriage counseling and the subject of children was discussed. Shirley even went into great details about the reasons why they needed to wait until they had been married several years before having children. Lenny had been very impressed with her explanation and he agreed with her. As far as Lenny was concerned, their marriage was over.

Shirley did not want the divorce and she was willing to do whatever she could to stop Lenny from filing for it. She made one last attempt to keep her marriage together. She told Lenny that she was pregnant with their child. Lenny was in shock and disbelief. With the news of him possibly becoming a Father, he began to reconsider the divorce.

Wanting to get a better understanding about Shirley and her need to lie, Lenny talked to Shirley's Mother, Ethel.

"I love Shirley but she had told me so many lies that I'm not sure we can make our marriage work even with her having my baby."

Ethel seemed surprised and asked, "What did you say?"

"You didn't know? Shirley's pregnant." Lenny knew from the look on Ethel's face that something was wrong.

"Oh Lenny. I'm not sure what to tell you." With sad eyes, Ethel was at a lost.

"Please Ethel. Whatever it is, please tell me. I need to know the truth."

"Shirley has always had a problem telling the truth and I don't know why. I'm sorry to be the one to tell you but it is impossible for Shirley to be pregnant with your child or any man's child. She had her tubes tied after her last child." Ethel's eyes were tearful as she saw Lenny's hurtful facial expression.

At that moment Lenny knew he had to get Shirley out of his life. Obviously, she had a problem and she needed professional help. As much as Lenny wanted his marriage to Shirley to work, he could not live a life of lies. As far as he was concerned, if Shirley could keep her children a secret and then lie about having his child, what else was she capable of doing?

The sound of a honking car startled him out of his deep thoughts. It was a good thing because he needed to leave or he was going to be late for his first golf lesson.

CHAPTER 7

Ebony watched her husband take a practice swing as though he had a golf club in his hand. With him being left handed, he looked awkward. She tried to stifle a laugh but it escaped her anyway.

"What's so funny?"

"Nothing but I wish I could be a little bird in a tree so I could watch you and Austin hit your first golf balls." Ebony said mischievously,

"I bet you would but it's not going to happen." Billy Ray Taylor gave his wife a playful hit on the behind when she passed by him.

"On a serious note, it will be great when you and Austin learn how to golf. Then we can have a foursome—You, Austin, Jessica, and me. We'll have lots of fun with the four of us golfing on the weekends or when we go on vacations."

"Well, don't expect too much from me. Although I played baseball, I've never been that athletic."

"Honey, you'll be a natural. Just wait and see. Generally, people that played baseball have an easier time than others transferring their skills to golf. Just don't let Austin or anyone else get under your skin."

"I'm not worried about Austin." Billy Ray stopped as he thought about the other men that might be taking the golf lessons. Usually Billy Ray was a confident man, but when he married Ebony, he found out how insecure he could be. His mind drifted off as he thought about his marriage to her.

He never expected to go through so many changes just because he married someone who did not reflect his image. His own family still had not accepted his wife. It had been three years since he had seen a member of his family. But it had been their choice. As a result, he was estranged from them. He had made it very clear to his family—if they could not accept his wife, then they could not accept him. That was just the way it was and he had no intentions of backing down off of his position.

If it had not been for Ebony's family accepting him with open arms, he and Ebony would not have experienced any type of family life. Ebony's father and mother treated him like he was one of their own. Although Ebony's parents never said it he was sure they were just as disappointed and concerned that Ebony had married outside of her race.

It was Austin who introduced Ebony to him. When he started dating Ebony, his family seemed surprised but Billy Ray did not think much about their reactions. However, when he announced that they were getting married, it was like he had committed a crime and he had been given a lifetime sentence in prison. His father's words still rang in his ears.

"What type of life are you going to have?" His father wanted to know.

"What does that mean dad?"

"You think you know it all. Remember when I tell you that the minute you marry that woman, your life is going to change forever."

Billy Ray did not fully grasp the impact of his father's words until he and Ebony were married. In many ways Billy Ray had been naïve. When he was dating Ebony either he had not paid attention or he did not care about the outside world and the amount of hatred and bigotry that still existed because of someone's skin color.

On television, in the newspapers, and in magazines, an impression was given that would make one believe that a lot of progress had been made regarding race relations. There was also the possibility that many people believe that there are little or no race problems. However, Billy Ray's experiences had caused him to think and know differently. Since marrying Ebony, it seemed as though he was noticing occurrences of prejudice daily. Then again, it could be that the bias was always there but he never paid much attention to it until he married Ebony.

The insensitivity of people toward people of color affected his life more than he expected. It seemed that regardless of where they went, he and Ebony could not escape the finger pointing, derogatory remarks, and sometimes even open threats from whites as well as blacks.

Billy Ray loved his wife and it was not until he married her that he began to understand racial attitudes. He would never pretend to fully comprehend every aspect of racial hatred because his skin was white, which gave him certain privileges that he took for granted every day.

With help from Austin, Billy Ray began to realize that most of the people who made any type of comments about race were ignorant. In many cases, these people had little or no contact with people who did not look like them. Austin was very patient with Billy Ray, teaching him coping skills for responding or not responding to finger pointing, crude racial remarks and jokes or idle threats.

When insulting remarks were directed toward he and Ebony when they were together, Billy Ray made every effort to remember Austin's words. *"Pick your fights because you can't win them all."*

Ebony had noticed that Billy Ray was off in his own world. She had not bothered him, however, it was time for him to leave to pick up Austin.

"Billy Ray."
"What?"
"It's time for you to get ready to pick up Austin."
"Okay. Listen, I'll see you later. I promise to behave myself.

Besides, your brother will be there to keep me straight."
 They kissed and Ebony watched as Billy Ray pulled out of the driveway.

CHAPTER 8

Jessica wanted to ask Austin about the golf lessons but she did not want to start his day off on the wrong foot. But she also wanted him to approach the lessons without worry. After much contemplation, she decided to broach the subject.

"I talked to your sister."

"Which one?"

"Ebony. She told me that you weren't that anxious about taking golf lessons. What's wrong?"

Watching her husband closely, Jessica wanted to make sure he answered her truthfully. She didn't want him to brush it off like it was nothing.

"That's not what…" He stopped talking and noticed that Jessica was looking at him.

"Okay. I have to admit I'm a little concerned about the lessons or should I say, I'm worried about Billy Ray."

"Don't get mad but sometimes you're overly protective of him. He's a grown man, so why the worry?"

"I know he's a grown man but I don't' think…know I know he never expected that there would be so much controversy because he married a black woman. With gentle reminders, I keep telling him that he has to pick and choose his fights." Austin shook his head.

"He can't fight everyone. After three years, he's doing better but he still has a tendency to let words and looks get under his collar."

Hiding her smile, Jessica shook her head. Hugging Austin, she said, "I know baby. It's hard. I know what we've been through but we made it and so will Billy Ray and Ebony."

Jessica could not resist adding, "I remember how you used to be."

Looking at him, Jessica did not have to remind Austin about how quickly he used to react to people making comments about them or the glaring looks. He tried to take on the world. As time went on, he found a balance of knowing what was important in life and that meant knowing when a man needed to defend a certain position and when he did not.

Jessica could understand Billy Ray's feelings. When you are white, you do not have to worry about being attacked because of the color of your skin. You assume acceptance without question. However, that is not true when you are a person of color.

It was devastating for her when she first started dating Austin. Then when they got married, it seemed like the comments and attacks got worse. It was like Austin had taken on additional harassment because he did not marry a *"sister."*

Being in an interracial relationship was difficult. There were still times when Jessica did not know how to deal with the racism she encountered because she was married to a black man. But overall, she learned how to ignore it. Jessica knew that in time Billy Ray would learn too, but it took time.

"If you're worried about the men who are taking the golf lessons reacting to Billy Ray being married to a black woman, just don't tell them that Billy Ray's married to your sister?"

Jessica waited for Austin to digest what she said. She wanted Austin to understand that it was not always necessary for him to tell people right away that Billy Ray was his brother-in-law.

"You're right." Austin looked at this wife and then smiled.

"There isn't any reason to tell these men that Billy Ray is my brother-in-law. Besides I know Billy Ray's not going to tell them he's married to my sister."

Pulling into his brother-in-law's driveway, Billy Ray looked at Austin and Jessica. Billy Ray admired Austin with his patience and skill to deal with all the gawking and comments he was besieged with for marrying a white woman. They were truly a happily, married couple.

Billy Ray worked with Austin at an accounting firm where both of them were managers. When he complained about how difficult it was to find a good woman, Austin introduced him to his sister, Ebony. There was an instant attraction between him and Ebony. No one thought they would get married except for Austin.

Having two younger sisters, Austin treated Billy Ray like the little brother he never had and Billy Ray loved Austin like a brother. Austin watched over him, making sure nobody messed with him and there was no way anyone was going to mess with his sister.

Billy Ray got out of the car and approached Austin and Jessica. He overheard them talking about their Sago Palm Tree.

"Austin, I think the tree has a fungus."

"Based on what?" Austin was looking but he did not see anything on the tree. It looked fine to him.

"See all the white bugs?" Jessica was trying to point the bugs out to Austin when she looked up and saw Billy Ray.

"Hi Billy Ray." Jessica gave him a hug.

"Billy Ray, right on time. How you doing and how you treating my sister?" Ever since Billy Ray married Ebony that was how Austin greeted him. Austin was sure to emphasize *"my sister."* It was a standing joke between them.

"I'm treating her the way you taught me or I know you'll give me a beat down." Billy Ray smiled and shook Austin's hand.

"How ya'll doing?"

"We're fine." They responded in unison.

Jessica said, "Billy Ray, don't let Austin tease you too much."

"Don't worry I'm going to ignore your husband."

"Man, you know I wouldn't be me if I didn't do some trash talking and joking. Got to go momma."

"Ya'll have fun. See you later."

Austin gave his wife a kiss. She waved as they pulled out of the driveway.

CHAPTER 9

The last thing Russell Allen wanted to do was to take golf lessons. But what could he do? His wife, Connie, signed him up for the lessons without telling him. When she told him about the lessons, she more or less told him in the form of a mandate. She did not give him an opportunity to say no to the lessons. Connie was an avid golfer and there were times when she expressed her desire for him to be able to golf with her. Since he really did not care that much for sports, he never wanted to golf.

However, for some reason, Connie had decided that it was time for him to learn. At the end of 40 lessons, Connie was guaranteed that Russell would be golfing. If not, she could get her money back. Although she had the money-back guarantee, he wondered what the consequences would be if he was unable to learn how to golf? There was no need for him to worry about that for now. At the moment, his concern was his children. He and Connie had fraternal twins—a boy and girl.

Whispering to his five-year-old twins, Russell Allen had stooped down so he could be at eye level while talking to them. It was important that they understood what he was about to tell them.

SUNDAY GOLF

Before he went anywhere, he always stressed to the twins, the significance of being on their best behavior. It was hard for the children to fully understand that their mother did not always have the patience when it came to loud noises and children misbehaving. Unfortunately, Joey and Joy did what children do and that was making noises, running and jumping, and talking and laughing loudly.

"You need to behave yourselves while I'm gone." Looking from Joey and then to Joy to see if they understood what he was saying.

He said, "Listen to your momma. Don't get in her way and do whatever she says. Okay?"

They nodded their little heads up and down to let him know that they understood. Russell pulled his boy and girl into his arms. Hugging them tightly, he wished he did not have to leave them. Releasing them from his grip, he looked at them.

Joey said in a quiet voice, mocking Russell's whisper. "We'll be good Daddy."

Softly, Joy asked, "Do you have to go?"

"I'm sorry Joy, but daddy doesn't have a choice. Momma paid for me to take golf lessons. So I have to take them."

In unison, they whined, "Why?"

"Because momma said so," he said firmly and then softened his tone.

"Come on guys, be good for me. I won't be gone that long." To say that he would probably be gone for about two hours would not mean anything to them.

They did not respond as they looked at their father with heartbreaking eyes. Their eyes said it all—they did not want him to leave them. To help the children remember to be on their best behavior, Russell used a little bribery.

"If you do not act up while I'm gone, we'll do something fun when I get back home. Okay?"

Their eyes shined brightly with anticipation. They began jumping up and down as they shouted.

"What are we going to do? What are we going to do?" They kept yelling as he tried to answer them.

"Please tell us Daddy. Tell us Daddy. Tell us Daddy." Excitedly, they pleaded in unison.

"Settle down now. If I tell you then it won't be a surprise." He smiled. He was glad to see the worried looks off their faces.

"It will still be a surprise. Tell us Daddy. Come on, tell us, please, please…"

Without warning, in mid-sentence, Joey and Joy stopped their pleading. Then they became still and quiet. Russell knew Connie must have been standing close by.

Sternly, she said, "I'm glad you stopped jumping up and down and yelling. You were making far too much noise."

"What was all the noise about anyway?" Bitterness dripped from her mouth as she looked at them.

"Nothing," Russell answered quickly.

"All that noise was for nothing." Glaring at Russell, she put her hands on her hips and waited for an explanation.

"Well, I was just explaining to Joey and Joy why I had to go out for a little while."

Russell looked up at his wife. He did not say anything else as he stood up. He did not want to irritate her.

"Well, you better hurry up or you'll be late." She was dismissing him.

For reassurance she added, "The kids will be just fine."

He looked down at their disappointed faces and said, "I know they will."

"Well, I better go." As he turned to leave, Connie added a word of warning.

"Don't do anything to embarrass me. I'll be checking up on you." Russell said nothing but he was startled.

"The instructor agreed to provide me with weekly progress reports regarding your golf lessons." Wickedly, she smiled.

Under his breath, Russell said, "Thanks for the added pressure."

"Did you say something?" She challenged.

"No," he lied.

"I'll see you later."

Russell kissed Joey and Joy good-bye. He made no attempt to kiss his wife.

CHAPTER 10

The sunny, warm Florida day matched Justin Williams' mood. Since his release from prison, every day was a great day because he had no one telling him when to get up, when to take a shower, when to eat, and where he could go. In addition, there were no bars clanging, to remind him that he was not a free man.

It was Sunday and he was pleased. It meant one more day before he would have to see and listen to his boss, who was also his father-in-law, Mr. Andrews. He was grateful for his father-in-law giving him a job because there were not a lot of employers willing to hire ex-cons.

However, it was not easy working for Mr. Andrews. It was like he was waiting for Justin to make a mistake to prove that he was right about his motives for marrying his daughter. In addition, he made no effort to hide the fact that he did not like him, nor trust him.

But along with the happiness, Sundays also brought emotions of sadness, disappointment, pressure, and guilt. Justin found religion in prison, but he never expected, nor did he agree to spend each and every Sunday in church—all day. Since he had gotten out of prison, he had not attended one church service.

SUNDAY GOLF

Each Sunday, Justin watched his wife, Suzanne's face. She hoped—no, probably prayed—that he would be going to church with her. Justin loved his wife but he also knew Suzanne was disappointed that he had not gone to church with her since his release, but she never pressured him about it. That was what Justin loved about her. Unconditionally, Suzanne loved him and gave him the space he needed.

In fact, it was Suzanne who suggested he find something to keep himself busy since he was not attending church. Watching so much golf on Sunday afternoons, he thought that it was something he might want to do. So, he decided to take golf lessons. After all, how difficult could it be?

Since being out of prison, Justin had found the adjustment to the outside world more difficult than he anticipated. It was just the little things—weekly he had to report to his parole officer; at random, he had to take a drug test; and there was the problem of meeting people. As part of his parole, he was not allowed to socialize with other ex-prisoners. It occurred to Justin that who ever thought of that rule was stupid. Why would he want to socialize with former prisoners? No, when he left prison, he had left that part of his life in prison. He did not want anything reminding him of his life behind locked bars.

Justin avoided telling people that he had been incarcerated. Generally, people were surprised to hear that he had spent time in prison. Then they became inquisitive. They wanted to know why he had spent time in prison, had he served all of his time, and on and on and on. As a result, Justin chose to keep his imprisonment to himself. Suzanne wanted Justin to be honest about his incarceration, especially when they socialized with people from church.

Justin tried to explain to Suzanne how naive she was about people. She assured him that he was to quick to judge them and that people from her church were nothing like he described. Regardless of how much she tried to persuade Justin that it was okay to confide in people from her church, he was not convinced.

It was difficult for him to forget the memories he had concerning the people from the church when he was growing up. The church people he had remembered were just as hypercritical as those not proclaiming to be regular churchgoers. Many of the church folks he could remember were very judgmental.

Sadly, he recalled his father who was a good man and had gone to church regularly. Life had beaten him down and unfortunately he ended up committing armed robbery. The people in church judged his father harshly. Yes, his father was guilty but he was trying to feed his family and with no skills and no job, he did the only thing he knew and that was—doing illegal activities. The church had a lawyer on retainer but refused to help his father until he was sentenced—20 years in prison. Then it was too late. That left a bitter taste in Justin's mouth. He trusted only one person in church and he was not a human being.

The crime Justin went to prison for was based on him thinking he could get something for nothing. He had done the crime and he had served his time. As far as he was concerned that chapter of his life was closed. Justin did not want to constantly discuss the whys, what ifs, and maybes of what he had done. He just wanted to get on with his life.

It was Suzanne's hope that Justin would help in the church's prison ministry program. She was optimistic that he would be a caring resource and could use his God-given talents to assist those similar to himself. However, Justin refused to enter any prisons for any reason. The painful memories of prison were too fresh for him and he wanted to forget.

From reading the newspaper while he was in prison, a lot of his friends that he had gone to high school with or lived in his neighborhood were either dead, on drugs, or in prison. In addition, most of the men he met or knew worked for his father-in-law. Those men were not high on his list for socializing or making them his friends. Justin did not trust the men he worked with and he suspected that the feeling was mutual. After all, he was the son-in-law and some of his co-workers knew it. That was why Justin was looking forward to golfing on Sundays. It might give him an opportunity to meet some men and possibly make some friends.

Justin was truly excited about his golf lessons. Perhaps, taking these lessons would be just what he needed to help him jump-start his life. Looking up at the clock, he realized it was time for him to leave. He did not want to be late for his first lesson.

CHAPTER 11

Stuart Bailey looked at his new recruits, as he liked to call them. This was a first. The entire class was made up of all men. Not one woman. This should be an interesting experience for him, as well as for the men taking the lessons.

Taking a moment, Stuart looked at the recruits. Instead of the men introducing themselves to each other, they stood off by themselves. The only two men talking were the white and black man.

"So typical of men." Stuart thought out loud.

Strolling toward the men, Stuart sized them up. He thought that on a whole, these recruits could be the most challenging class he had ever taught. Not because they were all men but because they all seemed to be in excellent physical condition. However, Stuart reminded himself that looks could be deceiving.

"Gentlemen, welcome to Tree Top Golf. The facility here offers a driving range and practice course. I assume that you all are here for your eight o'clock golf lesson." Stuart watched the nods.

"My name is Stuart Bailey."

Stuart stopped and looked at each man to emphasize his point. "My name is not Stu or Stewie."

"I live in Ocala. I've worked at Tree Top Golf for five years. To work here, each instructor must be a certified PGA professional. Not everyone who is an instructor participates in the local golf tournaments but I compete as much as possible. If you want more information about my background and qualifications, you can go in the golf pro shop. Furthermore, my credentials and bio are posted on the bulletin board, along with the other golf instructors that work here."

Stopping for a moment, Stuart continued. "Now, before we get started, how many of you have golfed before?"

Stuart looked to his right and to his left, not one hand was raised. It was hard to believe that not one of these fine specimens of a man had ever golfed.

"This is great—and a first. Everyone is at the same level which will make it easier for me when teaching the class."

Slowly, he looked at each man and finally said, "Before we start, I would like to have everyone come closer."

He motioned them to come toward him. As the men formed a tighter circle around him, he kept it informal.

"Now, I think everyone will be able to hear as we make introductions. To begin, I would like each of you to first give your name, second, where you live, and third, why you're taking golf lessons."

Without hesitation, a broad shouldered, dark skinned man of average height, wide smile and probably in his early 30's introduced himself.

"My name is Bob Webster. I live in Lady Lake. I'm taking up golf hoping to attract some different types of business clientele."

"I'm Justin Williams. I live in Wildwood. I'm taking up golf for fun."

Stuart was sure he was not the only one that noticed the biceps on this brother. He was truly fine with his bronze colored skin and light brown eyes. To go along with the biceps, Stuart was sure the man's golf polo shirt was covering up a well-chiseled six-pack.

"I'm Billy Ray Taylor. I live in Summerfield. I'm taking up golf so I can golf with my wife." That comment generated some laughter. From Billy Ray's slender frame and his height, Stuart guessed he was a runner. Billy Ray was not really handsome but yet his looks made him appear attractive. His looks reminded Stuart of the boy next door with his clean-cut look, light brown hair and blue eyes.

"My name is Austin Hayes, from Summerfield and I ditto what Billy Ray said. Billy Ray is my best friend and we want to learn how to golf so we can beat our wives."

Although Billy Ray was Austin's brother-in-law, they agreed not to mention the fact to the men. Billy Ray had enough pressure on him. He did not need the added stress of these men knowing that he was married to a black woman. Austin knew the attitude of some black men. They did not like the idea of white men marrying *"our black women."* Then again Austin was not sure how some of the men would react to him being married to a white woman.

The curious looks did not escape Austin when he mentioned that Billy Ray, a white, man, was his best friend. Purposely, Austin emphasized their relationship so if anyone thought they were going to mess with Billy Ray, they would think twice.

Stuart did not quite know what to make of Billy Ray and Austin. Maybe Austin was dating Billy Ray's sister or something. Without question, they were hiding something but Stuart did not know what. In due time it would come out.

Austin was good looking in a rugged way. His skin tone was more golden than brown set off with bedroom type eyes that were dark brown but looked almost black. His body was muscular, not like Justin, but you could tell he worked out.

Introductions continued. "I'm Woodward Roberts. Please call me Woody. I'm here because my wife made me." Again, most of the men laughed.

Stuart hoped Woody would not be a whiner. Stuart presumed he was the oldest man in the bunch. Woody looked to be in his late 60's or early 70's. Estimating Woody's height, Stuart thought he was about six feet tall and came from good genes because of the lack of aging lines and wrinkles. His skin was smooth with a tint of red undertones with high cheekbones. It was possible he could be a descendant from Native Americans. His hair was almost all gray with specks of black, here and there. From what Stuart could see, Woody did not have a hard body but he appeared to be physically toned.

Stuart asked, "Where do you live Woody?"

"Sorry. I live in The Villages."

"Thank you. Next."

"My name is Donnie Wilson. I live in Leesburg. I'm taking up golf because my company is having a golf tournament. So I won't make a total fool of myself, I want to learn something about golf before the upcoming event."

Curiously Stuart looked Donnie up and down. He was more than six feet tall, dark brown skin with beautiful straight teeth. From his muscular biceps, he looked as though he worked out on a regular basis. Stuart did not know why but immediately he suspected Donnie of being gay, bisexual, or perhaps he was one of those brothers who was married but liked to have sex with men—better known as the DL.

"I'm Lenny Harper. I live in Summerfield. I wanted to learn a sport I can do long into my old age."

Immediately, Lenny regretted he had made that comment. The dirty look Woodard Roberts shot him, said it all. Rather than apologize and make it worse, Lenny said nothing further.

Already, Stuart did not like Lenny. He was a nice-looking black man and he knew it. Looking at him, Stuart thought he could have been a model or a male dancer. From what could be seen, Lenny's body was well chiseled. His biceps were as if they had been sculptured rather than being powerfully built and his legs were more shapely than well developed.

"My name is Russell Allen. I live in Weirsdale and I'm here to learn a new sport," he lied.

The minute the words escaped his mouth, he knew it was a mistake. Stuart Bailey looked at him with a raised eyebrow.

Stuart could not stand a man who was controlled by a woman.

Connie Allen had called and talked his ear off regarding her husband. Mrs. Allen expected Stuart to provide her with a weekly progress report. Stuart resented the request because he was not instructing high school teens. Quietly Stuart complained because he knew how he made his bread and butter. The end result would be Stuart giving Mrs. Allen her requested weekly report.

Russell was probably six feet tall but a tad too thin. He was good looking in a schoolboy way. However, his eyes looked dead. Where life should have been in Russell's eyes, Stuart saw nothing but desperation.

At that point Stuart promised himself and he did not know why but he would do everything in his power to ensure that Russell learned as much as possible about golf.

CHAPTER 12

Glancing at his watch, Stuart could not believe they were already thirty minutes into the lesson and he had not provided these men with one golf instruction. The introductions had taken longer than Stuart had planned.

"Gentlemen. Thank you for reading my welcome letter, especially the part regarding the dress code. You must always wear a collared shirt, slacks or shorts. No jeans are allowed. Preferably, golf shoes, but tennis shoes can be worn. These rules apply even when you are hitting balls on the golf range." Stuart paused.

Since he saw no one raising a question he continued. "As you can see, your are a diverse group of men but you all have three things in common. One, none of you has an interest in playing on the pro circuit. Two, you all are here to learn golf, and three, none of you have golfed before."

Stuart stopped, looked at the men to see if there were any reactions. There were none, he kept talking.

"I can tell you that even though some of you have never golfed before, some of you will hit the ball like you have. For those of you that will hit the ball, don't get cocky. When you get on the golf course, it won't mean a thing if you can't hit the ball straight." Stuart stopped when he heard some heavy sighs.

"Then we have the athlete who thinks he should be able to play this game just because he is good at sports. Well to the jocks, you are in for a surprise of your life. You'll probably find that golf may be the hardest sport you have ever tried to learn." Stuart smiled wickedly as he watched the faces of some of the man.

"But gentlemen, do not let me discourage you. Golf should be and can be fun. Do not take yourselves too seriously because this is not how you will be making your money—only me."

Laughing, Stuart looked around. No one joined in the laughter; obviously they did not get Stuart's sense of humor.

"When you finally learn how to golf you will find that the real game begins when you reach the green. Other words, to be good, you must learn how to putt, but we're ahead of our selves. Gentlemen, let's get started."

Taking a poll, Stuart found out who needed golf clubs. He explained that anyone who did not have clubs could borrow clubs from the pro shop. Then he suggested.

"Everyone needs properly fitted golf clubs, especially when you learn how to swing the club. When you properly swing the club, ill fitted clubs will not reward you with a good golf shot. Anyone who plans on buying clubs can see me and I'll be more than happy to help you. With that said and everyone fitted with clubs, let's begin our lesson."

"Can anyone tell me what PGA stands for?"

"Professional Golf Association." Quickly, Russell Allen responded with a smile.

He was proud of himself for answering the question and hoped that Stuart would report that to Connie. He needed Stuart to provide Connie with as much positive feedback about him as possible.

"Correct Russell, but for all of you in this class, it means Position—Grip—Alignment. Every time you begin to hit that little white ball whether it is to tee off, chip, pitch, or putt—remember PGA."

Overall, the hour lesson went too quickly. The men's first golf lesson focused on PGA and Stuart showing them how to putt on the green. By the time the men started to practice what Stuart had demonstrated, the lesson was over.

Stuart gave the men drills and exercises to do before their next lesson. He said that he would know whether or not they were practicing them.

"The more you do what I tell you to do, the better you will be at golf. Remember what I said earlier, golf would probably be the hardest sport you have ever tried to learn. I'll see you next Sunday at the same place and same time. Have a good week."

Before anyone could say anything or ask any questions, Stuart had disappeared. The men gathered their golf clubs, said very little to each other, and walked to their cars.

CHAPTER 13

At a snail's pace, Lenny changed out of his golf shoes to a pair of sandals. Then, he put his golf clubs in the trunk of his car. Purposely, he was waiting for Bob Webster, who happened to be parked beside his car.

"Bob, do you have any plans?" Lenny was not sure why he chose Bob but he did.

Thinking for a minute, Bob considered his wife Nessa. He knew she would be pissed at the decision he was about to make but at the moment that was not his biggest concern. He needed some time alone. He wanted some companionship other than his wife.

Finally, he answered, "No, I don't have any plans, why?"

"Well, there's a Perkins Restaurant, not far from here on 27/441. Do you want to get some breakfast? I don't know about you but everything I ate before our lesson has seemed to evaporate. I'm hungry and need some food."

"Sure, I'll join you. You lead the way and I'll follow you."

Bob decided to leave his cell phone off, that way Nessa might think he was still engaged in the golf lesson. It was childish behavior but at the moment Bob was being selfish.

Fortunately, there were only a few people waiting to be seated in Perkins. Within ten minutes, they were ushered to a table. Looking at the menu, Lenny and Bob selected what they wanted quickly. When the waitress took their drink orders, they also placed their food orders.

Lenny and Bob had some things in common. They had both gone to Leesburg High School. Lenny graduated five years before Bob. They knew some of the same guys that played on the basketball team. Then, they discovered that they had gone to the same First Baptist Church when they were in elementary school.

"Man, it's a small world."

"You're telling me."

Their other interests included fishing, watching sports on television, and bowling. When it seemed as though they had nothing else to talk about, Lenny asked.

"What do you think so far about golf?"

"I don't know man. We didn't do that much. Although I have to admit that putting looks a lot easier on television than I thought. I have to say I was disappointed in that we didn't hit one golf ball. Next week, I hope we do more than just practice gripping the golf clubs, exercising, and listening to Stuart talk."

"Yeah, I was surprised that we didn't do more, but then we didn't have much time after all the introductions. But from what I can see I guess Stu knows what he's doing."

"You mean Stuart." They laughed.

"Man, I have to learn how to golf because my wife is a good golfer. She thinks it'll be good for our business."

"What kind of business do you have?"

"We own several real estate offices and we are trying to diversify. Right now, we are brokers and conduct closings but my wife thinks we should try and attract business developers and property owners. To have a diverse clientele helps out when the market for selling homes is slow."

"How will golfing help your business?"

"You know—decisions are made on the golf course. Besides, it's just another opportunity to meet and mingle."

"Oh. Well, I don't mean any disrespect but I'm glad I don't have that kind of pressure on me."

"Yeah, I know what you mean Lenny. It would make it a lot easier if I didn't have the added pressure of feeling as though I have to learn how to golf. Anyway, I'm going to try and not let it bother me. I've paid for the first 40 lessons and we'll see how it goes."

"I paid for the 40 lessons too but if I'm not getting it, I know at least I can quit. I'm merely taking up golf just to have something to do on Sundays." Lenny smiled at Bob.

Lightheartedly, Lenny said, "Who knows, golf might also be a way for me to meet some honeys."

Bob shook his head. He was so glad he did not have to worry about meeting women, dating women, calling women, and being rejected by women. Basically, Bob was glad he did not have to deal with the whole woman-dating scene.

The last thing Bob wanted to talk about was a woman. He had a wife who was probably madder than a baby who cries when wanting to be fed. He guessed he could call her but he didn't. Lenny seemed to be a down to earth guy but Bob did not want to talk about women. So he steered the conversation back to Stuart and their golf lesson.

"Since I don't know jack about golf, I don't know what to say about Stuart. However, he seems to be knowledgeable. I was impressed in how he explained the fundamentals of golf in very general, layman terms so we could understand. So, I'll just have to wait and see."

"I agree with you. He's a professional and I'm sure we're not his first nor will we be his last golf class. Let's face it; Stuart earns his living by giving golf lessons. With that money-back guarantee, I don't think he can afford to have many failures."

Lenny changed the subject but this time to something more personal. "How long have you been married Bob?"

With pride and a smile, Bob responded, "I'm a newly wed."

"Congratulations man!"

Lenny added, "I'm newly divorced."

"Congrats." Bob stopped short. He realized that congratulation was probably not the appropriate thing to say. In fact, he did not know what to say. So he said nothing as he cut a piece of pancake and put it in his mouth. Before silence made the situation awkward Lenny jokingly said.

"I know, what do you say to someone who's recently divorced?" Both men felt the strain but they laughed nervously. For some reason Lenny felt comfortable talking to Bob. He was enjoying Bob and their conversation. He seemed to be an okay guy, easy to talk to, and he had a sense of humor. Boldly, Lenny told Bob that it was his third divorce.

Coughing and spitting, Bob grabbed a napkin and covered his mouth. Bob had just put another piece of pancake in his mouth at the same time Lenny told him about the three divorces. Coughing several more times Bob finally regained his composure.

"Are you okay? Drink some water," Lenny offered.

"Lenny, the next time you care to drop something like that on me, could you at least give me some warning. Man."

Through laughter Lenny spoke, "I'm sorry Bob if I surprised you with what I said. I guess being married three times is a little shocking. What can I say, I like being married but I haven't found the right woman."

"It's okay but before I put anything else in my mouth or sip my coffee, do you have any more surprises?"

"Not really. That's pretty much my story."

Looking at his watch, Bob was flabbergasted. It was almost twelve o'clock. Nessa was beyond mad. Oh well, he would just have to deal with it. He had a good time and he would make it up to her.

"Look Lenny I need to go."

"I do too," Lenny lied. He could have stayed a little longer. He was enjoying himself. It had been a long time since he had had the opportunity to talk to another man with such ease. He talked to his male co-workers and had even socialized with some of them, but he had never shared any of his personal business with them.

They paid the bill, left a tip, and walked out together to the parking lot.

"This was great. I hope we can do this again."

"I'm glad you asked me Lenny. If this becomes a regular thing, I think we should ask some of the other guys to join us."

"That's a good idea. Take care. See ya."

CHAPTER 14

When Bob got home, the house was empty. He looked for a note from Nessa but there was none to be found. Talking out loud he commented. *"She must really be mad at me."*

Looking at the kitchen clock, it was ten minutes to two. He continued to talk out loud. *"It's getting late."*

Thoughtfully, Bob started pulling out pots and pans and proudly said. *"I'll surprise her and make dinner."*

Stopping, Bob decided to listen to some music. Looking through his CD's, he decided to go through his romantic music for couples—the Body and Soul Collection. Finding just what he wanted, he put the CD in.

Nessa loved Barry White. Maybe if she heard the deep sensual crooning of his voice throughout the house when she walked in, it might put her in a better frame of mind. At this point he knew he needed all the help he could get.

Getting out the whole chicken Nessa had put in the refrigerator to thaw out, Bob cleaned and washed it. He decided to cook Nessa's favorite recipe. Oh he was pulling out all the stops to avoid a confrontation. He did not want to argue. Humming to the music, he put the chicken in the oven. Setting the timer for two hours, he decided to relax.

Wondering where his wife was, Bob was restless. He was no longer interested in listening to mood music when his wife was not home. He turned off the stereo. Picking up the mystery novel he had been reading, he turned to the page where the bookmarker was. Usually, he had no problem reading a good book, but this afternoon he could not concentrate. He replaced the bookmarker on the page and put the book down.

Bored, he decided to occupy his time by finding something to watch on television. Picking up the remote control, he turned it on. Flipping through the channels, he found nothing that interested him. It always irritated him to pay the outrageous cable bill that offered lots of channels but yet he could not find a single thing to watch. Everything was either a rerun or something he did not want to see.

Turning to the cable movie listings, he decided to watch the Clint Eastwood cowboy movie, *Unforgiven*. Somewhere between when he laid down on the sofa and watching the movie, Bob had fallen asleep.

When Vanessa entered the house it was quiet except for the low chattering voices she heard. She concluded the voices were coming from the television. Quietly she walked into the family room. There napping on the sofa was her darling husband. He looked adorable curled up in the fetal position under his favorite fleece throw blanket. It took everything she had not to bend over and kiss his forehead.

As soon as Vanessa walked into the house, she recognized the wonderful aroma that had filled her nostrils. It was her favorite chicken recipe, chicken ala orange. Walking out of the family room, she went to the kitchen to check on the chicken. As she was about to open the oven door, she noticed Bob had set the timer to ensure that the chicken would not over cook. She smiled. It was sweet of him to cook dinner and make her favorite recipe.

It was hard being mad at a man who could cook. However, food or no food she was still angry with him. She was not going to let him off that easily.

Taking a magazine out of her tote bag, Vanessa headed back to the family room. She sat in the armchair opposite the sofa. Opening the magazine, she flipped aimlessly through the pages. She was not in the right frame of mind to read any of the articles.

The magazine was just a diversion while she waited patiently for Bob to wake up. In addition, she was trying to use the time to help her think about what she wanted to say to him. They needed to have a discussion, not an argument.

When the oven timer went off, Bob jumped. The beeping sound had startled him. Initially, Bob could not figure out what was making the loud repetitive noise. Then the aroma hit his nostrils as he remembered that he had put the chicken in the oven for dinner. Jumping up from the sofa, he was about to go to the kitchen when he stopped.

"Nessa, hi sweetie. I didn't hear you come in."

Slowly, she looked up from the magazine she was holding in her lap. She did not respond. A frown was on her face.

"I baked your favorite chicken recipe, chicken ala orange, for dinner. It should be ready. I was on my way to the kitchen to check on it. Can I get you something while I'm up—a glass of wine, water, soda?" He was rambling.

Again, she said nothing. She barely acknowledged him. If looks could be a weapon then he would surely be dead.

Deciding not to continue to attempt to engage her in conversation, he went to the kitchen. Checking on the chicken, he took it out of the oven. He substituted the rolls for the chicken in the oven. While he fixed a salad, Nessa joined him in the kitchen.

Whistling he got out the placemats, plates, silverware, and napkins. While he was about to set the table, Nessa started to talk.

"Bob..." Without warning, he heard a sudden outburst of sobs.

Putting everything down, Bob took the rolls out of the oven, and walked over to her. Hugging her, he smoothed her hair. Whispering in her ear, he told her how much he loved her.

"I'm sorry Nessa. After my golf lesson, I went to Perkins with one of the men. It was a spur of the moment decision. It's not like I deliberately planned to go. Then, time got away from me. I should have called you but I figured you'd be mad, so I..." He stopped as her sobbing eased.

"Bob…" Gently, Nessa pulled away from the embrace. She went to the kitchen counter to get a tissue to blow her nose. Rather than return to Bob's arms, she sat at the kitchen table.

"I don't know what's wrong with me. I don't care if you went to breakfast after your golf lesson. I think I was more upset that you blew me off. We were supposed to do something together, remember?"

Whining like a little boy, Bob made a sad face as he asked for forgiveness. "I know I was wrong. I'm truly sorry. I was home in time so we could have done something together, but you left and I don't blame you. You shouldn't be sitting around waiting for me. I'm also guilty of turning off my cell phone. Will you ever forgive me Nessa?"

"Bob, we're newly weds and I'm just trying to be a good wife. I think I'm trying too hard."

"Why try at all? I don't want you doing any more than what you were doing before we got married. You're my wife. Wife is just a title. Nothing more. Nothing has changed. I still love you."

The minute he made the comments he was not sure how she was going to react. But as he looked at Nessa's face, there were no more tears and Bob thought he detected the corners of her mouth had turned up into a smile.

"I don't know. I guess I thought to be a wife required me to do something different. I'm so stupid."

"No, you're not. Come here." Bob held her tightly and kissed her passionately.

Playfully, he asked, "Do you want to skip dinner and eat later?" Separating from their embrace, he looked deeply into his wife's eyes.

"What do you have in mind?" She flirted back.

Teasingly, Bob responded, "Let me show you, rather than tell you."

They laughed. All was well between them. Bob began to relax. Maybe now Nessa will get back to being herself.

It was Nessa who took the lead. Holding her husband's hand, she guided him to the master bedroom.

CHAPTER 15

If anyone asked the men, they would have admitted how disappointed they were with their golf lessons. According to the men, the lessons were going slow. The men were doing what Stuart told them to do but were getting impatient. It was hard for the men to tell if they were really learning anything because all they had been doing was listening to Stuart's lectures, watching some videotapes, exercising, and putting.

Each Sunday the men showed up at least 30 minutes before their lessons were to start. Diligently, the men practiced their putting in hope that Stuart would have them do something new and different, other than putting.

Stuart was always impressed to see the men practicing before their golf lesson. They were always productive while they patiently waited for him to arrive. Instead of the men standing around doing nothing, they did the drills and exercises he had given them, as well as helping each other. Stuart knew these recruits were going to be different but they had gone beyond his expectations. They were truly special. He wished all of his classes could be like these men. He knew the men were getting eager about hitting the golf ball but they were not ready.

When Stuart gave instructions regarding putting, the reaction was always the same. The men were disappointed. One Sunday, Stuart thought the men would be happy because he had them doing some different drills. The new drills involved Stuart teaching them how to practice short putts. He had them put a tee behind their putter, using the tee as a backstop. Then, he had them put a tee in the back of the cup and they had to try and roll the ball into the tee. Stuart tried to explain to the men that being confident and aggressive with their putts was the key to making them more consistently.

The men's faces equaled Stuart's displeasure as they showed their unhappiness. They wanted to hit the little white ball. However, what Stuart was trying to get the recruits to understand was that putting was probably the toughest part of the game. Putting was important because they had to learn how to commit to focusing their attention to seeing the ball go in the hole. If the men mastered putting they would possibly have more success at achieving birdies and pars.

One Sunday, Billy Ray was a brave sole and asked the question that all the men wanted to ask but were afraid.

"When do we get a chance to hit a golf ball?"

Stuart looked at Billy Ray as if he had been speaking a foreign language. Without responding to his question, Stuart proceeded to explain to the men other techniques regarding the art of successfully chipping and putting.

Billy Ray did not press the issue as he thought, *"he didn't answer my question."* However, he was not about to query Stuart any further regarding when they would be hitting a golf ball.

To end the lesson, Stuart demonstrated how the men could use different clubs for chipping the ball onto the green. He encouraged them to try using the "7 iron" to chip onto the green.

"If you use the "7 iron" the ball will roll more as it hits the ground. I suggest you practice this technique and it will be invaluable when you begin golfing."

Looking directly at Billy Ray, Stuart raised his eyebrow. "Are there any questions besides when you're going to hit the golf ball?"

Woody raised his hand. "Yes, Woody, what's your question?"

"Why is my back sore?" When Woody asked that question, all the men chimed in with the same complaint.

"It's possible that you're not standing over the golf ball correctly." So everyone could understand, Stuart demonstrated how to stand over the ball when putting to prevent a sore back.

Generally, Stuart was pleased with the recruits. No one was really grasping how to chip and putt better than anyone else. They were all progressing about the same rate. Stuart explained to the men that good putting required the right feel, reading the green, and having the right touch. Since none of them had golfed before, the men were hitting the ball too fast, too slow, too long, or too short. However, since the men practiced their putting diligently, Stuart knew that it was just a matter of time when it would all click for them. He could also tell that all the men were going to be better than average putters.

CHAPTER 16

After the Sunday golf lessons, Bob and Lenny continued to have breakfast at Perkins. One particular Sunday, Lenny and Bob waited for the rest of the men.

"Guys." Lenny had to shout. The men gathered around Lenny to hear what he wanted to say.

"Bob and I have been going to Perkins Restaurant for breakfast after our golf lesson. We wanted to know if any of you would be interested in joining us?"

Without hesitation, all the men excitedly accepted their invitation. He and Bob had discussed how many of the men might join them. They were betting on maybe four of the men joining them. But to their surprise and pleasure, all of the men would be going. That was beyond their expectations.

The first Sunday the men agreed to go to breakfast, Lenny stopped by Perkins before the golf lesson started and reserved the only table in the restaurant that could accommodate all eight of the men. The table was round. That made it easier for the men to see each other and the table made it more conducive for talking and listening.

Lenny thought maybe these men needed to talk to other men as much as he did. Although like most men, Lenny would never admit this need to any of them. To Lenny's surprise, that Sunday had set the pattern. After every golf lesson, all the men would meet at Perkins. To the men's satisfaction, Holly was their regular waitress.

She appeared to be young—may be eighteen years old. Despite her youthfulness, she was very efficient at waiting on tables. Holly always took and served their drink orders first. She never failed to bring out extra napkins. In addition, she made sure there was sufficient syrup and condiments on the table before taking their food orders.

Generally, the conversations were about sports, music, or local events, nothing heavy. As a rule one of the men would bring up a topic and from there everyone would give their opinions or comments.

However one particular Sunday, Billy Ray and Austin were whispering back in forth and were seemingly engrossed in their own conversation.

Annoyed Lenny interrupted them. "Are you two having a private conversation or can anyone join in?"

Austin and Billy Ray looked up, embarrassed.

Austin responded, "hey, my bag. We didn't mean any harm. We were discussing Stuart. I mean when is he going to teach us how to hit the golf ball? Is it just us or are you all disappointed as much as we are that we haven't been on the golf range to hit golf balls?"

All the guys responded, "yes" to Austin's observation and comment.

Lenny said, "Well, I don't think we're in a position to do anything about it."

Lenny looked at the men and asked, "Does anyone see how we can change what Stuart is doing?"

Before anyone answered, the food arrived. Once the food was served, the men did not get back to the conversation of golf until everyone had just about finished eating their food.

Russell interjected that he had discussed this with his wife and it seemed like Stuart was using the right approach.

Russell added, "My wife said that most men want to hit the ball long like Tiger Woods. What most men need to do is to learn how to chip and putt. My wife is an excellent golfer. Believe me. She knows what she's talking about."

Looking at Russell, Lenny noticed that when he first started talking, he had an abundance of confidence. Then when the men focused their attention to what he was saying, he reverted into a shy, timid man.

Woody added in agreement. "Basically, my wife said the same thing. My wife is on the golf course any time she's not working. So I think we're on the right track. I think what's bothering all of us is that Stuart seems a little unconventional in his teaching method."

Austin said, "Hmmm. You and Russell could be right Woody."

Billy Ray gave Austin a kick under the table. What Billy Ray and Austin did not share with the other men was that their wives had told them about the same thing. However, Billy Ray and Austin had not believed their wives, even though both women had been golfing for years and both had about a ten handicap. In fact, their wives probably could have taught them how to golf. However, both men and their egos were not about to let two women teach them a manly sport.

Then one Sunday the conversation turned personal. Bob knew it was just a matter of time before Lenny would get around to asking who was married. Everyone was married except for Lenny and Donnie.

That was about as personal as their conversation had gotten because Russell seemed uncomfortable either about talking about his personal life or it was about something else. The men thought Russell's behavior was peculiar. One minute he would be talking and then without warning he would announce he had to leave. Once Russell left the restaurant that usually caused the rest of the men to leave soon after.

Lenny was the only one who seemed disappointed that their breakfast outings ended sooner than he was ready for them to. For the first time in Lenny's life he felt as though he had been talking to men who were not judging him or did not want something from him.

CHAPTER 17

Closing the front door of his house, Russell felt something hard smash the side of his head. Before he could catch his breath, another blow went across his face. Then another whack landed solid against his body. He staggered back into the door, causing his head to snap back as his head hit the door hard. Russell's head was throbbing and his vision was blurred.

Slowly shaking his head as if to clear it, Russell looked around. Hearing his wife's voice, Russell was stunned beyond belief. Yes, he had experienced his wife's wrath before but this time he feared for his life as he saw Connie holding a baseball bat. Her voice had taken on an ear-piercing harsh, throaty, deep tone. Through piercing eyes, his wife was looking at him while thumping the bat against the floor.

"Where have you been? And before you answer, you better think long and hard."

"My golf lesson…"

"Liar."

This time her voice was loud as she screamed. "Now, where have you been?"

She repositioned herself as she put one hand on her hip. As

Russell looked at her, he thought about how she reminded him of his Mother, especially when he was a young boy and had misbehaved terribly.

"After my golf lesson, I went to…" Russell stopped as he felt Connie thrust the baseball bat into his stomach. He doubled over, gasping for breath. Punching him again, Connie waited. Trying to stand up, Russell felt his stomach churn as if he was about to lose its contents.

"Think again before answering."

Her voice was normal but as she continued, she shouted at him. "Where did you go?"

Waiting for him to answer, Connie's hand was beginning to hurt from gripping the baseball bat so tightly. She relaxed her grip as she watched Russell.

Slowly Russell opened his mouth to speak but stopped. He was in excruciating pain. For the first time since he was struck, he realized blood was surging from his lip and running down the side of his face. In addition, it felt as though one eye was swelling and trying to close.

Somewhere he had to summons up some inner strength so he could answer her. He was not sure he could sustain another blow to his body. Barely above a whisper, he answered her.

"I went to Perkins with the rest of the men after our golf lesson."

"Did I give you permission to go somewhere other than home after your golf lesson?"

Sneering at him, she roared, "You have been going to breakfast after your golf lesson for weeks. I have been waiting for you to tell me. However, you kept the breakfast meetings a secret. You should have asked me. I might have given you permission."

Pausing as if to catch her breath, she continued. "From now on, I expect you to come straight home after your golf lessons. Have I made myself clear?"

Out of the corner of Russell's good eye he spotted his precious babies. Gently closing his eyes, Russell wished his children did not have to see or hear any of this. They were crying and all Russell saw was panic on their faces and helplessness in their eyes.

She must have seen him looking at the twins because she yelled at them. "Quit that crying. Stop it, right now."

"Please God, don't let Connie turn her rage on them." Silently, Russell pleaded to a higher power for his children.

Then he got angry and thought. *"She better not lay a hand on either one of the children!"*

Connie's voice was full of impatience, venom, and hatred. "I'm waiting for an answer!"

"I think I need…"

Before Russell could finish his sentence, he felt another solid blow to his stomach. All the wind had been sucked out of him. The room went black and he crumpled to the floor.

CHAPTER 18

Looking through his left eye and slightly seeing through the slit of his right eye, Russell's vision was blurred. He did manage to see a woman dressed in green. He had no idea who she was. The woman was near his face and she was saying something.

"Mr. Allen…Mr. Allen. Can you hear me?"

There was ringing in Russell's ear, making it difficult for him to hear her clearly. His head was beating as if to keep in rhythm to a drum. In addition, he felt groggy. The woman was waiting. As much as Russell tried, words seemed to have been lodged in his throat. In an effort to communicate, slowly he nodded his head "yes."

"Good. You're awake. I'm Nurse Kendrick. Do you know where you are?"

Slowly, Russell shook his head, no.

"You're in the Leesburg Regional Medical Center. You're going to be okay Mr. Allen. You sustained a lot of bruises but the worst of your injuries was the cut above your eye. You had to get ten stitches. You also have a large, swollen lump on your head. The doctor explained everything to your wife."

Russell closed his eyes as he heard the nurse go on. "We'll be keeping you here over night for observations. We want to make sure you didn't have a concussion. We'll be moving you to a room as soon as one is available."

The nurse turned and left. Momentarily Russell closed his eyes again in hope that everything that he had just heard had been an out of body experience. Just as he was beginning to relax, he felt someone touching his shoulder softly. He opened his eyes. It was Connie.

"Russell honey. How do you feel? I've been so worried about you. Russell, the police want to talk to you."

Smooth, almost solicitous was the sound of his wife's voice. Before she could say anything else, two gentlemen were standing near the bed.

Confusion hit Russell as if someone had hit him with a large boulder. He could understand why Connie wanted to talk to him but why the police? He wished they would wait until tomorrow. All he wanted was to rest and to be alone.

"Mrs. Allen, would you mind if we talk to your husband?"

Connie tried her best to be pleasant as she said, "Please make it quick gentlemen. As you can see, my husband needs to rest. He's been through a lot."

"We're sorry and we understand but we really need to talk to him."

"Fine, but do you mind if I stay in the room with him? After all, I would like to hear what happened?" Hoping she sounded concerned, Connie left Russell's side and stood at the foot of the bed.

The two men looked at each other and shrugged their shoulders. The taller of the two men answered.

"Ugh…I guess. I can't think of any reason why you can't stay in the room while we question your husband."

"Mr. Allen, my name is Detective Donald Gray and this is Detective Jose Hernandez. We are with the Leesburg Police Department. We'll try to keep our questions brief."

Acknowledging the detectives, Russell must have moved the wrong way as a sharp pain went from the top of his head, down the side of his face, and settled at the bottom of his jaw line. Repositioning himself, Russell hoped the pain would subside so he could give the Detectives his full attention.

"Mr. Allen can you tell us how many men attacked you?"

Baffled, Russell did not answer immediately. In addition, he knew from the stern look on Connie's face he had better give the right answer. Slowly Russell began to speak through clenched teeth.

"To be honest...everything happened...so fast that...I don't remember much."

"Take your time Mr. Allen. Were there one or two men?"

Before answering, Russell looked directly at Connie for help. She provided him with the answer to the question. Carefully, she placed two fingers over her mouth. Russell understood. To anyone else it might have looked like she was just covering her mouth.

"There were two men."

Detective Gray asked, "Can you tell us anything else Mr. Allen?"

Before Russell could answer, Detective Hernandez asked several questions at once.

"Can you tell us how tall the men were? Were they Black, White, or Hispanic?"

Closing his eyes, Russell laid against the pillows for several minutes. Unhurriedly, he opened his eyes. Watching Connie, she shook her head. He was so tired of the lies; he felt a tear fall down the side of his face. He brushed it away. Biting the side of his cheek, he willed himself not to cry.

He could not envision what else he was expected to tell the police about the alleged mugging. One thing that amazed Russell about Connie was how creative she was when talking about how he obtained bruises and injuries. This time, it was if she had created a scene from a soap opera. He was wondering how it would end. Russell must have lapsed into a long silence as he heard the Detective state.

"Mr. Allen maybe we should continue this in the morning. With a good night sleep, something might jog your memory. Then perhaps you can give us a little more information about what happened."

Russell looked as though he was going to say something. However, seeing an opportunity to get rid of the police, quickly Connie spoke up before Russell could speak.

"Thank you officers. I really appreciate you waiting until tomorrow. As you can see my husband is in no condition to answer any more of your questions. He has been through quite an ordeal and the doctor gave him a sedative. He'll probably be asleep soon."

The police left. Connie felt a sigh of relief. She did not want Russell talking to the police alone until she had an opportunity to provide him with the story of what happened to him. She could not afford for Russell and her to be telling conflicting stories, therefore, possibly raising suspicion about his beating.

She could not remember a time when she had been so furious and disgusted with Russell. Russell was a big man and she did not anticipate him not being able to take a few light hits.

As hard as Russell tried, he could not stop the hurting. But yet, every time he closed his eyes it was if he had lost time. The last thing he remembered was being rolled down a hallway. When he opened his eyes, he was in a room. The room was set up for two people, but the other bed was empty.

CHAPTER 19

Russell's head felt as though he had eaten cold ice cream too fast. On top of that, he had the sensation that his head was spinning, like a toy top. He wished he had a way to stop it. Although his head was throbbing and he ached all over, his mind seemed to be in a hazy fog as he began to see images of Connie.

It was like his mind was rerunning events of long ago. There was Connie standing on the steps of her apartment building. That was when he first met her. Immediately, he knew she was the one. For him, it was love at first sight. On their first date what caught Russell's attention was her uncanny intellect. He was mesmerized by her ability to be able to discuss any topic, including current news events.

Matching her intellect was Connie's beauty. Before he met Connie, she had been a full figured model. Russell could easily visualize her walking down the runway with her almost six feet tall stature and her long, shapely legs. Her skin tone was unusual in that it was dark brown like a Hershey candy bar but with red undertones. To match her distinctive skin tone, Connie had the most astonishing light greenish-brown eyes, similar to cat eyes.

Her personality was likeable, sweet, and considerate. When she laughed, it was contagious. His family loved her and so did most people that met her. Connie was everything he could possibly want in a wife. After dating her for eight months, he proposed marriage and she accepted.

    Then the terror began. After about six months into their marriage, without warning, he came home late and Connie slapped him across the face. It was not a playful slap—more like a solid punch. Because she hit him with so much force, Russell suspected that he was going to end up with a black and blue bruise on his face. The next day when Connie saw the bruise, she seemed sincerely remorseful but she never said the words, *"I'm sorry."* She was more concerned about what they should tell their relatives, friends, and neighbors.

    Every slap, hit, and beating that left a bruise, Connie provided Russell with the details of how he got them. According to Connie, he was clumsy. He had a knack for tripping over his own feet or a toy, bumping into furniture, or falling down the stairs or a crack in the sidewalk. She had even convinced his family that he had been awkward and uncoordinated since he was a child.

    No matter how often he had bruises, not a single member of his family, friends, or neighbors ever questioned his clumsiness or the stories relating to the bruises. Most of all, no one ever suspected that Connie was the source of the bruises. Why should they?

    He was an independent medical transcriber for hospitals and doctors. As a result, he worked at home. This was Russell's only saving grace. By not working in an office, Russell was able to maintain some dignity. The bruises could heal without people gawking and whispering.

    Russell had tried to understand what brought about Connie's need to physically abuse him. However, after twelve years of marriage he still had no answers. At first Russell made excuses for her—she was under a lot of stress from her job, she was the first female manager for a large firm, she was juggling too many things—a career, children, a husband and making at least one business trip a month. It took years before Russell finally accepted the fact that there was no explanation for Connie's behavior except that she needed professional help.

There was never any pattern as to why, when, or how the abuse would occur. At the beginning of their marriage, Connie might have struck him once a week or once a month. When Connie was pregnant, she never touched him once. However, after the twins were born, the assaults became more frequent and violent. Most recently, the assaults on him had accelerated from occasionally to daily. The slaps, hits, and punches were always unexpected.

Russell thought that if he carefully watched and monitored what he said, how he said things, and what he did that he could some how prevent the assaults. Unfortunately, he found out that nothing seemed to work to stop Connie's physical attacks on him. Although he never defended himself against her, he would hate to think what he would do to her if she ever thought about raising her hand to either one of the children.

All the shelters he called or visited were for assisting abused women. Russell had not located one program that helped men. Another problem was persuading a counselor that his wife was abusing him. Without saying it, Russell saw the disbelief in the faces of counselors when he described the physical abuse he was experiencing. Although the counselors never said it, he knew the way they looked him up and down that they had difficulty believing that a man of his height and build could not defend himself from a woman.

What people did not understand was that Connie was strong and aggressive. He seldom had an opportunity to stop the assaults because she attacked him with unbelievable force. The attacks were always an element of surprise especially when she struck him with objects such as baseball bats, tennis rackets, or skillets. Once she started hitting him, he had little time to gain any strength to take the object from her.

It was true Russell could have fought back. However, if he reacted to her hits by striking her then he would have been no better than his wife. No, he had been taught that there was no situation when a man should raise his hand against a woman. Besides what type of an example would he be setting for his son?

He felt so alone. There was no one he could talk to. Even if he did discuss his situation with someone, from his experiences, he had no faith that anyone would believe him, let alone help him. Thinking now, he should have left before the children were born. But now, he felt compelled to stay. He was afraid to leave the children with Connie. He could not take the chance of her turning her anger and abuse toward them because of his actions.

Connie whispered in Russell's ear. "What were you thinking about?"

His face showed uneasiness. "You startled me."

"Why, are you that nervous?"

As she asked the question, Connie looked as though she was going to hit him. As a reflex, he jerked away from her. Not having much room in the bed, he grabbed the side of it so he would not fall out.

She laughed. "I was only going to fluff your pillow."

Connie's tone was silky smooth and tender. "How do you feel this morning?"

"Sore." Russell said *"sore"* but what he really wanted to say was—beat up. There were no words to describe how he felt.

"I'm so sorry you had to go through this. Those men could have killed you."

Sitting beside the bed, Connie patted Russell's hand. Bewildered Russell did not know what to say to Connie. So he said nothing as she continued.

"Russell, you don't remember but after your golf lesson you had to pick up some work from a doctor in an undesirable part of Leesburg. Since you didn't call to let me know where you were and it was getting late, I began to worry. So, I called the police."

She waited for Russell's reaction. Seeing none, Connie gave further details.

"After the police located you, they called me. Apparently you were a victim of a robbery. The thieves took your credit cards and money. With the drug problems today, people kill for almost any price. It's a miracle, you're still alive." Stroking Russell's arm, Connie looked tenderly at him.

"You were really lucky this time." Emphasizing each word, Connie was making a point.

Every nerve in Russell's body froze. Connie was giving him a warning. Had her bullying gone from beating to killing? It was one thing to be a victim of domestic violence but it was another thing to wonder if you are going to be killed. She did not have to worry about her message; he understood it loud and clear. Before Russell could respond to Connie, the police detectives from last night appeared in the doorway.

"Mr. Allen, how are you feeling this morning?" It was the detective named Donald Gray who was asking. Russell was so used to the lies concerning his abuse that it was easy to pick and choose what to say based on the information Connie told him.

"I'm just glad to be alive officer. I'm sore and have a few bruises but I didn't sustain any real injuries. With time, I'll be fine."

"Well I'm glad to hear that. Now, by any chance do you remember any more than what you told us last night?"

"Not really. I guess I was just in the wrong place at the wrong time." Russell looked pitiful.

"Well, Mr. Allen, you might want to reconsider whether you want to continue doing business with that particular client."

Russell nodded his head as if to agree with the detective. For one fleeing moment, Russell thought about telling the detective what really happened. Then as quickly as the idea entered his head, it left when he saw Connie staring at him. It was as if she knew what he wanted to do. With a watchful eye, she listened closely as he began to speak.

"I guess without any more information it's difficult to catch the person who might have committed this robbery?"

"I'm afraid so. Without any descriptions or information, it will be almost impossible to find your robbers. That is unless someone saw something." Russell perked up. Maybe there was hope after all until the detective said.

"Which I seriously doubt because people normally do not want to get involved when a crime has been committed."

"I see. I wish I could be of more help. I just don't remember."

"Well in case you do, I'll leave my card." Before Russell could receive the card, Connie had reached out and took the card from the detective.

"Mr. and Mrs. Allen, have a nice day."

The detectives left. Although Connie had her back to Russell, he could have sworn Connie was smiling. Russell had more reason than ever to fear for his life.

CHAPTER 20

Looking in the mirror, Russell barely recognized himself. Touching his face, it was painful and swollen. The bruises were no longer black and blue; they had taken on a purplish hue. Where he had the ten stitches above his eye, the area had dried into a brown-crusted film. The lump on his head was no longer protruding but the area was still sore to the touch. He definitely appeared as though he had been in a street fight or had been in the boxing ring with Mike Tyson, the professional boxer.

The last thing he wanted to do was to take his Sunday golf lesson. As time went on he resented telling the imaginary mugging story regarding his bruises. He was feeling like a little child who was not really sick but yet did not want to go to school.

"Russell, you better hurry up or you're going to be late for your golf lesson."

He started to yell to answer Connie but then thought better of it. So he walked to the kitchen where she was sitting, reading the newspaper.

"I thought I'd skip my lesson today. With my bruises and all…" His voice faded off.

Before answering him, she folded the newspaper neatly and put it on the table. She looked directly at him.

"Don't be ridiculous. There's no reason why you can't go to your lesson. Suck it up. Quit acting like a little boy who was in a fight and lost. Don't forget, I've paid for the lessons and there are no refunds."

Glancing at Russell, she seemed to have an idea. "I think you should go to Perkins and join the men after taking your lesson."

Puzzled Russell let Connie continue. If nothing else, he had learned over the years not to interrupt her while she was talking and not to second-guess her.

"You need to try and bond with some of the men. That is, if men bond."

She laughed for a minute, stopped, and then proceeded.

"I'm sure that when you share with the other men that you were robbed, they'll not only understand but one of them will probably have a story of their own." She uttered a laugh again.

Russell was getting annoyed with Connie. It took all his will power not to show his anger. When Russell looked at his wife, he could not believe it but from her laughter and facial expressions, he thought she was actually enjoying the fact that he would have to explain to the other men how he got his bruises. He found nothing amusing.

Glancing at the clock, Connie reminded Russell that he needed to go or he was going to be late.

"We'll see you later Russell. Have a nice time."

Connie's voice was full of ridicule. "Oh, and I suggest you don't be late."

CHAPTER 21

Any other time, Russell would have arrived early to talk to the men, exercise, and practice. Today, Russell was not only the last one to arrive, but he showed up about five minutes before the lesson. He only had enough time to do some quick exercises and no time to practice. Immediately, Lenny noticed Russell's bruises.

"Man what happened to you? You look like Sammy Davis, Jr. tap danced on your face."

"When we go to breakfast after our lesson, I'll explain it to everyone then."

If Stuart had not walked up at the same time when Lenny asked him what happened, he would have told him, but Russell did not trust Stuart. Russell was not sure how much Stuart told Connie about the lessons. Therefore, the less Russell said in front of Stuart, the better off he thought he would be. Stuart could not miss Russell's bruises but did not question him about them.

"Okay gentlemen, let's get started today. Guess what?" No one answered.

"You're going to learn how to hit the little white ball. This is what some of you have been waiting for." Stuart smirked and looked at

Billy Ray.

Between the laughter and agreed nodding heads, the men gave high fives to each other. Stuart knew that most of the men were anxious to hit the golf ball but until that moment, he had no idea how much it meant to them.

"Let's get started. To hit the ball, you must take a full swing." Stuart demonstrated.

"Taking a full swing is similar to putting and chipping. The difference is that you will make a bigger motion."

Billy Ray asked, "what about your stance?"

"That's a good question. You need to spread your feet so they are shoulders width apart. You do that basically for balance." Stuart showed everyone and asked that they try it.

"When taking a full swing, you are making a motion away from the target and back to the target. Now, let me see what you got."

The men soon discovered that hitting the white ball was not as easy as they had expected. As the men tried to hit the golf ball, Stuart was continuously emphasizing certain instructions.

"Keep your head down. Keep your eye on the ball, if you want to hit it." When Stuart was not making those two points then he was saying.

"Control your speed. Not so fast. Take a nice easy, rhythmic, controlled swing."

Last but not least Stuart told each one of them over and over again. "You don't have to kill the ball to hit the ball."

When the lesson was over everyone let out a sigh of relief. Lenny and Billy Ray were the only two who seemed to be able to hit the ball straight and with any regularity. The rest of the men hit the ball either to the left, to the right, or they hit the ball just enough so the ball dribbled only a few feet in front of where the ball had been teed up.

At breakfast, the men were louder than usual and almost everyone was complaining about the lesson. In addition, some of the men grumbled about their forearm hurting.

It was Lenny who watched Russell. He seemed to be in deep thought. His mind certainly was not on the golf conversation. In fact, he had said very little since they arrived and made almost no comments about the golf lesson.

Rather than beat around the bush, Lenny came right out and asked. "Russell now that we're at breakfast, how did you get the battle scars?"

"I was robbed," Russell said grimly.

"Robbed. No way." Austin exclaimed.

"Where?" Austin asked.

"Leesburg. I don't know exactly where. In fact, I don't remember a lot about what happened."

Eying him, Justin asked, "Why don't you remember what happened?"

"I was told by the doctors that I suffered a…" Russell stopped and threw up his hands.

For some odd reason he decided to tell the men the truth about Connie. After all it was her suggestion that he have breakfast with these men. He did not know the men that well but then again he could not think of one male friend that he had. So what did he have to lose? Shaking his head, Russell exhaled a loud breath of air.

"I wasn't robbed. My wife kicked my ass." His confession caused complete silence, shock of disbelief, and inquisitive looks.

Lenny inquired. "You're joking about your wife right?"

Defensively Russell replied, "No, I'm not joking.

"Why would I joke about something like that?" He waved his hand over his face.

"We're sorry," said Donnie sympathetically. He glared at the other men.

"Go ahead, tell us what happened," urged Donnie.

"Thanks man." Thinking for a minute he wondered if he should go into details about Connie beating him or just give them the high points.

Austin asked, "Russell, are you okay?"

"I'm okay. It's just that I don't know where to begin…I mean…"

Several of the men encouraged Russell to begin by telling them what happened with the most recent bruises. Russell sat for several moments before continuing.

Finally, he divulged his well-kept secret. "She's abused me almost from the beginning of our marriage. I've put up with it because I was taught you don't hit women. In addition, I have two children."

When he looked at the men, he knew that what he said did not make much sense. Tears were beginning to well up inside of Russell.

Silently he prayed, *"I can't cry. Not in front of these men."*

Several times he cleared his throat as if to ward off the threatening tears that were about to come forward. From the looks on the men's faces he could tell they thought he was pathetic and now he was doing everything he could to hold back tears.

Clearing his throat, he weakly mumbled, "This was the first time I ever ended up in the hospital. From what my wife told me, when I passed out from when she beat me earlier, she waited until dark and then drove me to an alley in Leesburg. When she stopped the car, she shoved me out the door. Then she called the police, saying that I had not come home from my golf lesson and she was worried."

Billy Ray questioned his story. "Well, if you don't remember anything, maybe you were robbed?"

"No! I wasn't robbed. My wife beat me up. She made up the fictitious story about me being robbed." Defiantly Russell answered.

"When your wife first beat you, why didn't you go to the police?" Woody wanted to know.

"And say what?" Russell snorted and looked hopelessly.

"Man, I'm sorry but I'm not going to let any woman beat me, not like that. Yeah, I've been taught not to hit women too. But man I'd have to teach her a lesson at least one time!" Billy Ray did not hold back when he commented.

"Yeah man. I mean we're talking about a woman. I understand you not wanting to hit her but this is over the top. I mean I wish my wife, Jessica, would hit me. After one time, she would think twice about raising her hand to me again. Man, you're acting like you got sugar in your tank." Austin's comment was similar to Billy Ray's as he shook his head.

"What does that mean?" Russell asked.

"You know, like a faggot." Austin's voice did not hide the disgust he felt.

The other men began making similar comments. It seemed like the other men had been waiting for someone to be brave enough to make a comment about Russell's wife beating him. When Billy Ray and Austin made their remarks, it was like they had opened a jar of honey and the bees began to swarm. Everyone had a comment or a strong opinion as to how Russell could stop the wife beatings.

Donnie was not sure if anyone had noticed but he had said very little. It might be hard for the men to believe Russell but Donnie could see it happening. Donnie thought about some of the women in his family. They are not just big but they are aggressive. He could see one of his female cousins beating a man. He wanted to say something but with him being gay he feared the men would automatically label him as being a "faggot" or being light in the loafers, with no backbone. Yes, he was "gay" but that did not mean he was weak as a man.

Looking at his watch, Russell knew he had to go. He didn't dare be late.

"Look fellows I really...look, forget about what I said about my wife." Russell was sorry he ever mentioned it. Looking around the table at the men, Russell could not remember a time when he felt so worthless.

Donnie thought Russell was more courageous than he would have been. He would have left way before now. Not to mention, he would have cursed a few of the men out. Some of the comments were down right rude and cruel. Not to mention, that some of the remarks were not necessary. Donnie thought Russell looked so dejected when he left.

"Well fellows, weren't we understanding and supportive?" remarked Donnie forcefully.

The men looked at Donnie, but no one said anything.

CHAPTER 22

Driving home, Justin felt guilty. Thinking of his own situation the last thing he would have wanted or needed would have been a bunch of men making rude comments about him being in prison.

Why hadn't he defended Russell? Why hadn't he been supportive of him? Justin knew the answer to those questions but he did not want to admit that by keeping quiet, he did not have to expose himself.

Justin knew it must have taken a lot of guts on Russell's part to tell them that his wife beat him up. After all what man would want to tell other men that he was being beat up by a woman, on a regular basis,. When Justin thought about it, all he could think about was that they acted like a bunch of teenage boys. Better yet, they acted like the typical macho man.

Anyway, Justin decided that he had to help Russell in some way. When he got home, he would talk to Suzanne. After all, her paid position at the church was to counsel and help abused women. Why couldn't she help an abused man?

Justin thought how every one of those men probably had a secret but not every man would have the balls to tell it. He admired Russell for telling his story because he knew how reluctant he was to tell people that he had been in prison.

Entering into the house, Justin was glad to see that Suzanne was home. Walking into the kitchen, he watched her for a few minutes. He truly loved this woman. If it had not been for Suzanne, he was not sure if he would have survived doing his entire prison sentence.

Originally, he had five years but with Suzanne's support and her strong belief in God, she was able to get his prison sentence reduced. It took two years to work the system but he was freed after doing three years of his five-year sentence.

When Justin was released from prison, he was only supposed to call Suzanne for resource or employment information. However, he knew he wanted to get to know her better. After six months, he got up enough nerve to ask her out. At first, she was very professional in refusing his advances. Finally, she relented. The dating led to friendship, love, and then marriage. It was the best thing that ever happened to him.

"You scared me." Suzanne squealed and looked up at Justin.

"Hi."

"Why didn't you say something?"

"Because I was too busy admiring my beautiful wife. What are you doing home already? I know church didn't let out early?" He smiled and then let out a laugh.

"Smarty. I decided to skip out early to be with you. I was hoping you'd come home early."

They embraced and Justin kissed her tenderly. Against her friends and family's counsel she had married Justin. In the five years she had been doing prison ministries, she had never been or allowed herself to be attracted or emotionally involved with any of the prisoners or ex-prisoners. When she thought back—there had been some "fine" looking brothers who she could have easily fallen for but she thought it would have been too risky. That was, until Justin.

There was something about him. He did not try to run a con game on her. She had found him to be trustworthy, considerate, and willing to admit he had committed a crime and should have been punished. Continuously, he apologized for what he had done and was willing to change his life.

"Suzanne, why don't you sit down and let me cook you something?" Justin did not know what was bothering Suzanne but he knew her well enough now to know when she had something heavy on her mind.

Suzanne did not know how to tell Justin that she was pregnant. That was the last thing they needed. When she had brought up the subject of children once before he was adamant about not wanting them. She had been on birth control pills. They had been careful but she must have been one of those 99 percentiles that did not get the full protection from getting pregnant. Since she was pregnant she thought it must have been God's will which meant to Suzanne that she was carrying a very special baby. When the doctor told her she was pregnant she was shocked, delighted, and petrified. Her loving husband would not be pleased but she had to tell him soon.

"Earth to Suzanne…"

"I'm sorry what did you say?"

"I said, sit down. I'll cook you something to eat. I've eaten. After our golf lesson, the brothers…I should say the guys because we do have one white guy, Billy Ray, go to Perkins. At first I didn't want to join the guys but the more time we spend together, the more I'm enjoying being with them. We talk about a lot of things and…" Justin's voice trailed off.

Excitedly, Suzanne said, "I'm so glad you're meeting some men."

"Maybe you'll be able to make some friends." Suzanne knew that male company was a missing ingredient in Justin's life. He needed some male friends and that was one reason she was glad he started taking the golf lessons.

"We'll see. I don't have any high expectations. Right now the only thing I have in common with those men is learning how to golf."

As he put the eggs in the skillet, he could not help but notice Suzanne's facial expression. He saw the hurtful look but he had not intended his tone to sound quite so callous.

"Not to change the subject but I want to discuss something with you Suzanne."

"You sound so serious. What's wrong?"

"Oh. Everything's okay, it's not about us or me. It's about one of the men whose taking golf lessons. He came to the lesson today with bruises. When we asked him about them, he said his wife beat him up. With your experience have you ever heard of a woman beating up a man?"

Suzanne did not respond right away. She was trying to recall a time in her career when a man had asked for help because of his spouse physically abusing him. None came to mind.

"Personally, I have not dealt with a woman beating up her husband but it could happen. Abuse can be in all forms. You have men beating women, men and women beating children, children beating children, and children beating parents. So as you can see, why couldn't a woman beat a man? Anyone can be abused."

"Well, if it's true, this man needs help and I don't think he knows where to get help or who would help him. Someone asked him about going to the police but he said they generally didn't believe…"

Suzanne interrupted Justin. "I'm not surprised. The police still have a long way to go regarding spousal abuse. With all the educational material available, the police are still reluctant to get involved in what they call "domestic" abuse or violence. What do you want to do?"

Justin put his hands up and replied. "Oh, I don't want to do anything but I thought maybe you could help him."

"Justin, why don't you help…" Cutting Suzanne off in mid sentence he responded.

"Look. I want to help the guy but the other guys…"

"This is not high school. This is real life. This man needs your help. Forget the other men and help him." His wife was dismayed at him.

"That's okay." She went to her purse and pulled out one of her business cards.

"Here, the next time you see him, give him my card. In the meantime, I'll see what I can find out in the way of resources for him."

SUNDAY GOLF

Suzanne knew Justin was having a hard time adjusting to life outside of prison but she had hoped that he would be able to go beyond the "me" factor. She would continue to pray for him, her, and their unborn child.

CHAPTER 23

Sunday golf lessons were going well for all the men but the 40 lessons were just about over. They were extremely excited about their last lesson. Stuart had told them that they would be golfing on an 18-hole golf course.

The breakfast outings had become as much a part of their Sunday routine as their golf lessons. Since Russell had told the men about Connie he had made it a point to exit as soon as the lesson was over.

When one of the men asked him about going to Perkins, he made an excuse for not joining them. Usually, he told them he had other commitments. Then he would tell them that maybe he would join them next Sunday.

So far, Justin had not had the opportunity to give Suzanne's business card to Russell. From what Justin could see, it did not appear as though Russell had recently suffered from any new beatings. After the golf lesson, Justin confronted Russell about going to Perkins.

"Russell, are you coming to Perkins?"

"I don't know Justin. I mean…"

"Look Russell, you know the guys didn't mean anything by their comments. You know how men can be. Why don't you join us today? And if you still feel uncomfortable then you don't have to go any more."

"Okay. I'll see you at Perkins. Save me a seat by you, okay?"

Justin would save Russell a seat but he was not sure this was the man he wanted as his friend. Than again, maybe God was testing him. Anyway he would try to give Suzanne's business card to him today. According to Suzanne, if Russell's wife was abusing him then it was just a matter of time before she would do it again.

As usual the men got their same table in the rear of the restaurant and Holly was their waitress. Everyone was surprised as well as glad that Russell had decided to join them at Perkins. Since it had been Billy Ray and Austin who had come down the hardest on Russell, Justin was grateful when Billy Ray and Austin said they were glad to see him. That seemed to break the heavy tension that was hanging in the air like smog.

Woody seemed somewhat subdued as they ordered their breakfast. It was Lenny's uncanny instinct that made him notice and he asked him what was wrong.

"It's my wife. You all are too young to be going through what I'm experiencing." Everyone disagreed and laughed.

"Yeah what makes you so sure?" Bob asked Woody.

Woody shrugged his shoulders.

"As long as you're married to a woman or involved with a woman, sooner or later, she'll put you through something or other." Everyone agreed with Bob.

Once everyone settled down, Woody said, "No this is different. I don't even think women like to talk about the "M" word."

"What is the "M" word?" Bob quickly asked.

"Menopause."

"Okay but are you going to explain why it's making your life so miserable?" Bob was curious.

"That's what I'm trying to tell you all. Menopause is the change of life for women and it's hell for the husband. One minute this woman is sweet and adorable, and then she's like the wicked witch of the West from the Wizard of Oz. My life has been turned upside down."

"You mean that's what I got to look forward to? I love being married but it's been tough. I mean I have found it hard adjusting to all the mood changes."

The look on Bob's face was one of dread and concern. He had no idea about menopause and at what age women start to go through it. With Nessa's mood swings—he wondered if she could be going through menopause? That would certainly explain some of her behavioral changes.

Billy Ray commented and asked, "The medical field always has drugs. What about drugs?"

"Please. A recent study was completed and it was found that hormones aren't safe. So there are no drugs to help. Did I tell you about the hot flashes?"

In disbelief, Austin asked, "You mean those are real?"

"That's putting it lightly. She's hot, she's cold and then at night there are times when our bed is so wet that we have to get up and change the bed. I'm so glad I'm retired. There are some days when I'm totally exhausted because of the lack of sleep. If I was working, I don't think I could handle it."

"Why don't you go and talk to her doctor or go on the Internet and become knowledgeable about the subject?" Russell gave that recommendation.

Woody did not answer Russell because he was not interested in doing any of that, he just wanted his wife back—the one he originally married. He was sorry if he was painting a grim picture of menopause but it was no walk in the park.

Menopause was horrific, along with being much older than his wife. Woody did not dare tell the men how her sex drive had escalated and he was having a hard time keeping up with her. He did not want to hear the comments these young guys might make. He remembered all too well what he and some of his buddies used to say to some of the older men with younger wives and now he was in the same position. He could not stand to hear those same words he had once uttered. *"Maybe what you need in the bedroom is some help from a younger guy."*

Donnie waited to see if Woody was going to say something else. When Woody didn't, he interjected.

"I feel sorry for women. They go through so much. If men had to endure half of what women went through, we wouldn't make it. I know I can't imagine having a baby or the monthly thing."

Billy Ray was nodding in agreement. Donnie could not believe it. Usually Billy Ray was the one who usually took the macho viewpoint but this time he seemed genuinely concerned about women and their issues.

"My wife has a terrible time with her monthly. I feel so sorry for her and I feel so helpless."

"Billy Ray I can identify with that. Jessica has a terrible time with cramps too."

"Gentlemen, can we please not go there. I'm trying to eat my breakfast. I feel for the sisters but I guess we just have to grin and bear it." Lenny wanted to change the subject.

Without warning Russell jumped up. His facial expression looked as though he had committed a crime and was about to get caught.

"I had no idea it was so late. I've got to go."

When Russell stood to leave, Justin announced that he had to go too. Russell and Justin said their good-byes and left. Out in the parking lot Justin gave Suzanne's business card to Russell.

"I hope you'll use it. I think my wife can help you. If she can't, she'll find someone who can."

Russell knew he only had a business card, but for some reason he felt for once maybe there was some hope. Not knowing what to say, Russell said nothing and got in his car and sped off.

Russell could not believe that he was running so late. He had been so careful about getting home at his appointed time. He had gotten so involved in their conversation that he had lost track of time. When Russell arrived home, he prayed Connie would not notice that he was late.

As quiet as possible, he eased the door close. When he turned around, he saw the tennis racket coming toward him. Without hesitation, he raised his arms up in defense, trying to protect himself. He felt the full force of the whack on his arms. Again and again, the tennis racket hit against this arms. Then he heard a cracking sound. He prayed that neither one of his arms were broken.

CHAPTER 24

As Mandy prepared to make the telephone call, she prayed Lenny was not home. Dialing the number, she heard the phone ring—once, twice, three times. Her prayer had been answered. But instead of leaving a message on his answering machine, she lost her nerve. Quickly, she hung up the phone.

Why was she being so cowardly? To be fair to Lenny, she should have told him to his face that she could no longer see him. However, she feared that if she saw him she would lose all decency and would end up in his arms and then in bed. So, she took the uncomplicated way out.

It had been weeks and Lenny had not heard from Mandy. He did not have her home, cell, or office telephone numbers; as a result, he always had to wait for her to communicate with him. When he thought about it, Mandy had been in complete control of their relationship—affair. He did not even know her last name. For all he knew, Mandy was not her real name.

If he was truthful with himself, he knew that the last time they were together he was never going to see her again. Why had he pushed so hard? From the beginning, he had known she was married and she had no intentions of leaving her husband.

Getting the mail from the mailbox, Lenny thumbed through it. Mostly junk mail and then he saw a letter. In the space where there should be a return address, there was a hand drawn heart and the name, *"Mandy."* His heart started racing. Quickly, he opened his front door; he rushed in, threw his other mail on the table, and sat down in the nearest chair. Taking the letter out of the envelope, he began to read it slowly.

Dear Lenny,

I hope you're doing well. As you can see, I'm taking the painless way out. I don't have the courage to face you. After our last meeting, I could tell I had to end this affair now, before someone got hurt. I certainly did not intend to hurt you.

We both knew what the affair was all about when we first started it. From our last meeting, I felt your feelings were beginning to get involved. I could not allow that to happen and I could not afford or allow myself to hurt you. I've already hurt my husband but he just doesn't know it.

I cannot continue seeing you. However, you did bring joy, support, and understanding into my life at a time when I needed it. I will miss you and hope you can find true love in the future.

Always,
Mandy

Lenny reread the letter and felt like someone had stuck a knife through his heart. The pain was more severe than he anticipated. It had only been minutes since he read the letter but already he was touched by the emptiness.

The letter should not have been a surprise but for some reason he was caught off guard. From the first day the affair started, he knew that at any given moment he could hear the words that would "end" the affair.

One more time with Mandy, that was all he wanted. But who was he kidding if he were to see her again he would do everything—beg, plead, and yes even cry if necessary in order to keep her in his life. But Lenny did not have to worry about doing any of those things because he would never see her again. Wanting her to be happy and wanting what he wanted, Lenny knew it was a stalemate situation. Simply put, he thought he had found his soul mate but obviously that was not the case. Therefore, there was no way she could ever be his.

CHAPTER 25

"Hello Ebony. This is Billy Ray's mother."
Ebony could not believe her ears. Billy Ray's mother was on the line. Hesitantly, Ebony responded.
"Hello Mrs. Taylor. How are you doing?"
"I'm fine. Is Billy Ray home?"
"No ma'am. As we speak, he's probably on his way home."
"Well, can you please have him call me as soon as he gets in?"
Ebony was about to answer her but the phone went dead. She had hung up. Well, for the most part, Billy Ray's mother had been civil. Billy Ray's mother did not tell Ebony what she wanted and she did not ask.
The traffic was heavier than usual. Finally, Billy Ray was home. Driving into his driveway, he was happy to be home. It had been an exhausting day and he was tired. The tax season was always gruesome but that was how he made his living. He was thankful that the tax season only lasted a few months out of the year. To ensure that everyone's taxes were completed without errors and extensions filed on time Billy Ray had been working at home into the wee hours. He hated this time of the year but what could he do? When the April 15th

deadline date was over, Billy Ray and Ebony would fly to Jamaica for some rest and relaxation—that's what motivated him.

Ebony heard Billy Ray pull into the driveway. When Billy Ray put his key in the door lock, he was surprised when the door opened. Ebony was standing there with a big smile on her face. Ebony very seldom met him at the door. Billy Ray welcomed the sight of his beautiful wife but he knew something was up. They embraced and kissed. They closed the door and went inside the house.

"How did you know that I needed a kiss and a hug?" She shrugged her shoulders.

"What's up? You look like the mouse that got away from the cat."

"Your mother called," Ebony gushed.

Billy Ray's response was not what Ebony expected. She thought he would have been thrilled but instead he was unresponsive.

"Did you hear what I said?"

"Yes. What did she want?" Billy Ray's voice had a tint of bitterness. His family had hurt him badly. So he did not have any expectations about his family members.

"I don't' know. She just made me promise that I would have you call her as soon as you got home from work."

"So call her," Ebony urged,

"After dinner," Billy Ray replied.

"Billy Ray call your mother now." Ebony did not tell Billy Ray, she directed him as she handed him the phone.

"Dial the number." Ebony stood over him while he dialed the number.

Punching in the number, he hoped secretly that no one was home. However, at the end of the third ring, he heard his mother's voice, instead of the answering machine.

"Hi Billy Ray. How are you?"

When Billy Ray heard his mother's voice, he stiffened as she asked him how he was doing. It was like he had been talking to her every day or once a week. Inhaling and exhaling, Billy Ray hoped he could keep all traces of hostility out of his voice.

"I'm fine momma. How's everyone?"

"That's why I'm calling. Your father is in intensive care. He had a heart attack."

Watching Billy Ray's facial expression closely, Ebony could tell something was seriously wrong. Not wanting to interrupt his conversation, she listened intently trying to get the jest of what his mother might be telling him.

"What happened?"

"He was at work. He was found sitting at his desk. No one noticed him immediately even though he was slumped over. From what I was told, he was near death. What saved him was one of his co-workers gave your father CPR until the ambulance arrived."

Billy Ray heard a muffled moan. Before he could say anything, he heard his mother speaking again.

"I should have known something was wrong because earlier that morning he was complaining of indigestion. I sort of ignored him because lately he seemed to be whining about all types of aches and pains. I dismissed his complaints. After all, your father isn't getting any younger. Aches and pains is a part of growing older. Then, to top it off, he wouldn't go to the doctor when he did complain about his symptoms." Billy Ray's mother had gone off on a tangent and he had let her. Evidently, she needed to vent.

Clearing throat sounds, sniffling, and the sound of his mother blowing her nose, Billy Ray suspected she was crying. He should have said something comforting, but no words would come forth.

When Billy Ray heard his mother speak again he could only think about when he was a little boy. Her voice would be so loving and warm but then without warning she managed to deliver bad news. It was like the time when his dog was killed by a hit and run driver. His mother interrupted his memory.

"Billy Ray, I know we have had our differences but…what I'm trying to say is that your father is asking to see you. Can you come home?"

"Oh momma this is the worse time of the year for me…" The minute he said those words he wanted to take them back.

He was a manager for a large CPA Firm. Yes it was the tax season and he had been taking work home from the office, but his staff was more than capable of taking care of things if he needed to visit his father. If he was being truthful, he wanted his father to feel the pain he had felt all the years of him rejecting him and his wife.

The silent moments went from seconds then to minutes. Finally his mother said in a low, barely audible voice.

"I understand." She hung up before Billy Ray could say anything else. He hung up the phone saying nothing to his wife. He was numb.

"Billy Ray what's wrong?"

Trying to answer Ebony, Billy Ray could only feel heaviness and then constriction. Trying to compose himself, Billy Ray inhaled deeply and then exhaled noisily.

In a matter of fact tone, he said, "My father had a heart attack and he wants to see me."

Again Billy Ray exhaled and his tone was unsympathetic. "I'm sure the only reason he's asking for me is that he thinks he's dying. Knowing my father, I suspect that if he thinks he's dying and being the Christian that he claims to be, he needs my forgiveness if he wants to get into heaven."

Ebony wanted to admonish him for saying that but she knew how Billy Ray's family had treated him. She thought this was the time for his family to learn how to forget and to forgive. Life was too short.

"What's wrong with your dad wanting to atone for his sins?"

Ebony not waiting for Billy Ray to respond continued. "When are you going home?"

"I'm not."

"Oh yes, you are. Don't stoop down to your father's level. An eye for an eye and a tooth for a tooth isn't what it's cracked up to be. While you pack your bags, I'll go on the Internet and find you a flight."

Billy Ray knew Ebony's tone all too well. She had just given him an order and she expected him to obey it. Sternly, Billy Ray replied.

"Ebony, I'm not going. Just because a person's dying…" Interrupting his sentence and pointing a finger at him, Ebony told him with conviction.

"You're flying to Maryland and you'll stay as long as your mother needs you."

Walking over to the sofa where Billy Ray had been sitting, Ebony sat on the sofa arm, beside him. She reached out and hugged him. At that moment, Billy Ray could no longer control his emotions. Uncontrollable sobs came forth and tears fell down his face. Ebony put his head on her chest and softly stroked his hair.

"Go ahead, let it out."

CHAPTER 26

"Hello."
Immediately, Austin recognized his sister's voice. "Hi Ebony."
"What's up?" Ebony went straight to the reason why she was calling.
"Billy Ray's father had a heart attack. As a result, I doubt that Billy Ray will be back in time for the Sunday golf lesson."
"I'm sorry to hear about his father. How's Billy Ray doing?"
"As best as can be expected. After all, this is the first time in three years that he has seen his family."
"Maybe the two of them and the rest of the family will make peace before anything happens to his father."
"That's why I didn't go with him. I truly hope Billy Ray, his father, and his family can finally forget and forgive. If not, and if Billy Ray's father dies, he'll live with guilt the rest of his life. Not to mention I'll feel somewhat responsible."
"Hold on. It's not your fault. They're ignorant people. Don't blame yourself. You've tried and so has Billy Ray to make things right with his family and that's all you can do. The rest is up to them."
The last thing Ebony wanted to discuss with Austin was Billy Ray

and his family. She changed the subject.

"How are the lessons going? Billy Ray hasn't said much about them. He does talk about you all going to breakfast at Perkins. From what he's told me it sounds like you all have a good time."

"I have to admit I enjoy the camaraderie we have after the golf lesson each Sunday."

"I'm glad for the two of you. In fact, I'm glad for all of you men. Men need to talk more. You know bond."

"Whoa I'm not sure that's what we're doing. All I know is that we're a bunch of guys having breakfast after taking a golf lesson." Austin replied defensively.

"Whatever." Ebony could not understand why men hated to appear soft. That was what she liked about the new "metro sexual" men. They aren't afraid to get in touch with their feminine side.

"Not to change subjects but are there any single men in that class?"

"Why?"

"Duh. Your baby sister, Eloise."

"What about her?"

"Come on Austin. There isn't one single man in that class?"

"Well, Lenny is single but he's been divorced three times. Then there's Donnie whom I suspect is on the DL, you know down low or gay. Which one do you want me to introduce to Eloise?"

"Listen, we're talking about Eloise. She needs to meet men and we need to help her. No one said anything about marrying anyone. Besides just because Lenny's been married three times doesn't mean he's not a decent man."

"Is Eloise that desperate?"

"Who said she was desperate?"

"You did, when you said that Lenny may not be that bad a catch even though he's been married and divorced three times."

"Well, what about the other man…ugh the one on the DL?"

"What about him?"

"Did he tell you he was on the DL or are you guessing?"

"A man just knows these things. Trust me, if he's not on the DL, then he's sweeter than honey."

"Fine. Then the DL guy is out but at least give the divorced man Eloise's number. They're adults. Once he gets the number, they're on their own." Austin didn't say anything.

"Do it for me, please?"

"Okay I'll give him the number but only if I get the opportunity." Austin agreed unenthusiastically.

"Before I give him the number, I'm going to warn him that my sister is a beautiful, independent, aggressive, bullheaded, arrogant woman."

"Oh no you won't. You are only to say that Eloise is a beautiful, independent, opinionated woman. You can leave out the rest."

Even though Ebony could not see Austin, she knew he was teasing and she could tell from his voice that he was smiling.

"Please, don't tell me that I didn't describe your sister?"

"Let's say she knows what she wants and knows how to go about getting it."

"That's your interpretation."

"Whatever. Look. I got to go. If I hear anything from Billy Ray, I'll let you know. Don't forget to give…"

Austin cut her words off. "Okay. I love you sis. Take care and tell Billy Ray to hang in there."

Although Austin told his sister he would give Eloise's digits to Lenny, he wasn't sure he would do it.

CHAPTER 27

When they hung up, Austin was hoping for selfish reasons that Billy Ray made it back in time for Sunday's golf lesson. When he thought about it, he really had not had that many conversations with most of the guys. He would be on his own Sunday.

Maybe he would give Eloise's number to Lenny after all. It would serve her right. The last time he tried to fix her up with a brother the poor man got his feelings crushed and a broken heart. If only she would soften her approach. Her motto was "do it to him before he does to me." Eloise had allowed one bad experience to serve as a measurement for all men. As a result she classified all men as no good, cheating dogs. Sometimes he wondered if his sister put him in that category.

By Sunday, Billy Ray had not returned from Maryland. According to Austin's sister, Billy Ray did not want to leave until his father had been taken out of the intensive care unit. The doctors seem to think that his father would have a full recovery. In addition, he would need lots of rest and rehabilitation. Not to mention his father would have to make some major life changes such as diet, exercise, and work. The doctor suggested that he might want to consider

SUNDAY GOLF

retiring, cut back on his working hours, or work part-time.

Austin and Stuart arrived at the same time for the golf lesson. Austin gave Stuart a short version regarding why Billy Ray was not present.

Stuart passed out a flyer before the lesson began. The flyer provided the directions to Baseline Golf Course.

"Austin, will you please take one for Billy Ray?" Austin acknowledged Stuart with a nod. He handed him the flyer.

"Everyone, please remember to bring your clubs and go directly to Baseline. Although we do not need tee times, we should plan to arrive early to ensure that we get the earliest tee times available. Does anyone have any questions about Sunday and what we will be doing?" Hearing nothing Stuart went on.

"Good let's get started with today's lesson. Basically, we're going to be reviewing information we'll need for golfing on the golf course."

The lesson went fast and everyone was excited about golfing next Sunday. They were going to be golfing on an actual golf course. After the lesson, everyone headed to Perkins.

When they arrived Justin sat beside Russell. Justin did not say anything but he noticed Russell had on a long sleeve shirt. The sleeves were not quite long enough to cover his entire arms. At the wrist, it was hard not to miss the black and blue bruises. Justin was sure Russell probably had bruises all up and down his arms.

Russell leaned into Justin and whispered. "After breakfast, Justin do you think, we can talk?"

"Sure. We can eat and split out early. How's that?"

"Great. And thanks."

The men placed their orders and everyone wanted to hear about Billy Ray and what happened to him. Austin put his fork down.

"Billy Ray's father had a heart attack. He flew to Maryland where his father lives."

"How's his father doing?" Woody asked.

"He's doing better but he's not out of the woods yet."

"Well, is Billy Ray going to make it back for the last lesson?"

Justin asked.

"I hope so. Thanks everyone for your concern. I'm sure that will mean a lot to Billy Ray." Austin was really appreciative that the men sounded concern about Billy Ray.

"Let's talk about Billy Ray for a minute. How did you and Billy Ray meet?" After Lenny asked, he looked at Austin closely.

"We work together." Austin's answer was a slight too quick.

"Oh, and that works out okay? I mean…I ask because not many white people, especially men socialize with brothers after work hours."

"Yeah I know what you mean but Billy Ray is cool."

"I didn't say he wasn't cool but you have to admit, he isn't the typical white man. Could it be that you and Billy Ray are more than just close friends?"

"What are you insinuating?" Austin responded defiantly.

Not waiting for a response, Austin quickly got Lenny's meaning. "Oh hell no. You think we're gay?"

"I didn't say that. I mean…"

"Listen Lenny, did you forget, we're both married."

"Yeah but with so many men on the DL…" Lenny threw up his hands.

"We're good friends, period." Austin looked directly at Lenny to make sure he understood.

"I suggest you move on to another topic," Austin said.

Austin could have put a stop to Lenny's and perhaps the other men's speculations regarding his relationship with Billy Ray. All he had to do was to tell the men that they were brothers-in-law. But Austin did not and he was not sure why he did not tell them. One thing for sure, it was none of their business.

"What if they were gay?" Boldly, Donnie asked as he stared at them.

"What's the big deal?" To Donnie's disappointment his voice cracked with the second question as everyone stared at him.

Justin said, "I can't speak for anyone else, but I don't have a problem with anyone's sexual preferences as long as they don't try to hit on me. Then we have a problem."

"Look, I don't have any gay friends and I don't want to start having any now." Woody was adamant.

"How would you feel if a white person said that about you? Do you realize how prejudice that sounds?" Russell said.

"I don't care how it sounds. I have a right to pick and choose my friends. Faggots aren't my choice." Woody defended and some of the other guys agreed.

Donnie's skepticism of these men had just been confirmed. They did not even want to know that gay men are no different from straight men.

"But you're making assumptions and decisions about gay men without getting to know the person."

"Whatever, but I stand behind what I just said. Besides I don't want anyone thinking that I'm gay."

"Please Woody. Just because you socialize with a gay man doesn't make you gay."

Disgusted Donnie rolled his eyes and added. "So many straight men are so homophobic."

"Why are you so defensive about…" Woody gasped and squinted at Donnie.

"Oh my God. I should have suspected it. You're one of them. You're gay, aren't you?"

Before answering, Donnie looked at each man, unflinchingly. "Does it make a difference?"

Woody felt as though Donnie had deceived them. Confidently, Woody spouted. "It might."

"Give me a break." Taking a deep breath, Donnie spoke directly at Woody.

"Up until now, everyone was cool with me as long as you thought I was straight. But now that you know I'm gay you have a problem with me. Fine, if that's the way it is, I'm out of here."

Donnie stood up to leave.

"Sit down Donnie." Until that moment Bob had been the only man who had made no comments or voiced an opinion one way or another. Glancing at Bob, Donnie sat down and listened.

"You're cool with me. How can I say anything negative about you? You see my brother is gay. If everyone would admit it, we all probably have a relative or a friend who's gay but we keep it under wrap—a secret hidden in the closet. Praying and hoping that no one will find out."

Slowly, the table grew quiet. There was no further discussion of Donnie's sexuality because Austin changed the subject. He started talking about them golfing at the Baseline Golf Course. From the looks on everyone's face, they seemed relieved to talk about golfing.

When Russell announced that he had to go Justin also left with him. When they left, Lenny wondered out loud.

"There's something going on with those two. I'm not sure what it is but I'm sure we'll find out sooner or later."

"Are you implying..." Woody stopped.

"Never mind. Why don't you just mind your own business?" Bob admonished Lenny.

Outside of Perkins, Russell got right down to business. "I never got a chance to thank you for your wife's business card. What I want to know is there a good time that I can call your wife?"

"Call Suzanne any time. I'm used to people calling her at all hours. You see when people are in trouble they don't pick the time of day. Trouble happens twenty-four seven. As a result Suzanne has made herself available, day and night."

"That doesn't bother you?"

"Not really." Justin looked at him and shook his head.

"You see Suzanne helped me when I thought I had sunken to the bottom and didn't have a clue as how I was going to get up. In fact, she was my saving grace. Although she would say, it was God, not her." Justin could not begin to explain to Russell how Suzanne had been and still was the most powerful, influence in his life.

"I admire you Justin."

"Don't admire me. I was just trying to help a..." Justin wanted to say *"friend"* but it stuck in his throat. He smiled. Russell was his friend whether he wanted to admit it or not.

"Well, I appreciate everything you're doing for me. Thanks for everything."

"You got it. Look man. You better get going."

At that moment Justin felt good about himself. This was the first time since he had been released from prison that he had allowed himself to be vulnerable. He could not recall how long it had been since he had been honest with another human being. It felt good lending a helping hand to someone in need and expecting nothing in return.

CHAPTER 28

"Billy Ray, I don't expect you to forgive me but I am asking you if we can try to be father and son again."

"Dad I appreciate you wanting us to mend our relationship but what about my wife, Ebony? I mean she's not going away. She's my wife and I love her. To have a relationship with me, means accepting my wife."

"I'm not going to lie to you, I was taught that interracial marriages were wrong."

"But you and momma always taught us to see people as people. You always said not to judge people by the color of their skin."

"Yes, and I meant that, but we never thought you would marry someone other than a white girl. I'm sorry. I guess we should have made it clear about how we felt about you marrying someone outside your race."

"But you didn't…" Billy Ray could feel the tears welling up. Turning away from his father, Billy Ray stared out the window.

"Son, listen to me. Your mother and I can accept Ebony but it's the fact that she's your wife that's difficult to swallow. As a Christian family we were taught that "likes"—birds with birds, dogs with dogs were supposed to be together and that also applied to same race."

His father's breathing was uneven when he stopped talking. Quickly, Billy Ray turned around to make sure he was okay. Seeing that his Father was doing all right, he turned back to the window.

His father took a sip of water and continued. "I must admit that as a Christian, it isn't right for families to be apart. As a result, as a family we are going to have to pray for God's help and ask for his wisdom and guidance regarding your marriage. But you need to understand that the rest of the family will probably never accept Ebony."

Billy Ray turned around to face his father and said, "I don't care about your brothers, sisters, and my cousins. I just care about my immediate family—you, mama, Susie, and Ronnie."

"I understand. But it won't be easy." That was not the answer Billy Ray wanted.

"Do I have a choice?" His response came out rough.

"Look, that's the best I can do. If we are to start mending our relationship then we need to be as honest as possible. Do you understand what I'm saying?"

Nodding his head "yes" was the only reaction Billy Ray gave his father. Billy Ray understood what his father was saying but it was disappointing. However, it was a start. Because of his father's health, Billy Ray did not want to upset him or push too hard. He said nothing further.

On the plane, Billy Ray thought about his family. He truly wanted his relationship with his Father and family to work, primarily for Ebony. She was always saying what would happen if she got pregnant.

He could hear her words clearly. *"Our children will never know but one set of grandparents."*

Picking Billy Ray up at the airport, Ebony was so happy to have him home. During their phone conversations Billy Ray had not said whether he had made up with his family, but she was sure they had come to some sort of understanding. She was excited for him as well as for them.

She and Billy Ray had a good, solid marriage but she knew he missed his family. Before they got married Billy Ray had a close relationship with his family. But when they got engaged and then married, it was like they had committed a sinful act. When Billy Ray asked Ebony to marry him, he did not realize that marrying outside one's race to his parents and family was just like breaking one of the Ten Commandments. What Ebony couldn't understand was that these were—church going people. They believed in the good Lord, but they did not believe in interracial marriages.

Before they got married, Ebony and Billy Ray had a discussion with his family. Ebony tried to explain to Billy Ray's family that everyone's blood had been tainted. During slavery there was so much intermingling that most people had black, white, red, brown, and yellow blood. In fact, Ebony told them that if they were to research their genealogy, they would probably find out that mixed blood probably already existed in their family. It did not matter to them that Ebony was Native American on her mother's side and her grandfather was half white.

Intellectually, they understood what Ebony was saying but they just could not face the idea of having mixed grandchildren. Ebony even told them that when she bled, the color of her blood was red, just like their blood. They still would not accept her.

Billy Ray opened the car door and put his suitcase in the back seat. Climbing into the front seat, he greeted Ebony. "Hi sweetness."

He asked, "have you been waiting long?"

"Not really. I just got here."

"Good. Can I get a kiss before we leave?" Ebony leaned over and they kissed passionately.

"I missed you baby."

"Billy Ray, I missed you too. Now let's go before we get a ticket for indecent behavior."

On the ride home Billy Ray told Ebony all about his visit. Then Billy Ray said the unexpected.

"My parents invited us to spend Memorial Day weekend with them. Since my father is not allowed to travel and I said that I might visit them over the holiday, they suggested that you come with me."

Excitement flowed through Ebony's body and then apprehension. The weekend would definitely be stressful. However, she was willing to do whatever it took to help Billy Ray and his family to get back on speaking terms.

"Are we staying at your folks' house?"

"We don't have to but since they invited us I don't see how we could stay any where else." Billy Ray saw the worry lines on Ebony's face. She did not have to worry he would not allow his family to do anything to hurt her. He hoped she knew that.

He changed the subject. "Did Austin say anything about the golf lesson?"

"He didn't tell me anything but he's going to introduce Eloise to Lenny. What do you think about that?"

Billy Ray's eyes widened. It was not that Lenny would be a bad catch, but to introduce him to Eloise. He was not sure that was a good idea. Eloise understood all too well what it meant to say, *"there's a thin line between love and hate."* She loved men and yet she hated them too. Billy Ray had a good relationship with his sister-in-law and he wanted to keep it like that.

"I can't believe Austin agreed to introduce Eloise to Lenny."

"Well, he said he'd give Eloise's number to Lenny."

Shrugging his shoulders Billy Ray said nothing further about Eloise. He could not wait to talk to Austin about it.

CHAPTER 29

"Billy Ray, welcome back man. How's your father?"
"He's doing much better. Thanks for asking. If all goes well, he will be released from the hospital later on in the week."
"So everything's straight between the two of you?"
"Sort of. We'll see. Ebony and I are going to visit my folks over Memorial Day weekend."
"You're kidding?" Austin was surprised.
"No, my parents suggested it." Without Austin saying a word, Billy Ray could feel the concern through the phone.
"Don't worry I won't let anybody do anything to hurt Ebony."
"I know you won't. I'm happy for you and my sister."
"Well, it's a start. What did I miss at golf, or should I say what did I miss at Perkins?"
"Nothing really." As he stopped to think about it, he added.
"Woody ousted Donnie into admitting that he was gay."
"Well, that was a no brainer. From day one, you and I said he might be sweet."
"Well yeah, but for him to admit he was homosexual was something else. No one expected that. After that, the conversation got somewhat touchy."

"Anything else?"

"Sunday is our last lesson and if you remember, we will be golfing on an 18-hole golf course. We're going to a course named Baseline. It's located in Belleview. Do you want me to drive?"

"If you don't mind. Since I've been back, work is killing me and I'm a little tired from…"

"Don't go there! You forget that's my sister you're talking about."

Billy Ray laughed. Then paused for a minute.

"I forgot to ask, what's this I hear about your sister Eloise. I understand you're playing matchmaker. Tell me you didn't fix Lenny up with Eloise."

"Yeah, but it's not like that. I merely gave Lenny her number. Then, I told Eloise that if and when Lenny called her, they were on their own. I don't want to know anything about them dating or other particulars. The last thing I want is to be a part of a love triangle. You know how crazy my sister and your sister-in-law can get. I still say my parents brought the wrong baby home from the hospital."

Again Billy Ray started laughing and he could barely talk as he asked, "What's new with Russell? Any new stories about his wife beating him up?"

"Nah. He hasn't said anything, but he looked like he had some new bruises. He did his best to hide them. It was nearly 80 degrees and he had on a long-sleeved shirt, trying to cover up the black and blue bruises on his arms. I feel bad because I didn't believe his story about his wife abusing him. It's still hard to believe that a woman could be doing this to him."

"Lenny thinks something's going on with Russell and Justin." Austin stopped for a moment to get Billy Ray's reaction. He said nothing.

"Like what? Don't tell me they're on the DL?"

"No man. I don't know what he was getting at."

"Oh well. Listen. I got to go. Thanks for the updates. I got work to do, in and out of the bed."

Austin playfully said, "Thanks for sharing Billy Ray."

CHAPTER 30

The Baseline Golf Course was plush and green. The golf course was lined with a variety of different trees. They seemed to be everywhere on the course's fairway. To help Stuart with the last lesson, he had brought along one of the certified PGA instructors from Golf USA.

"Guys, this is John Cherry. He's going to be assisting me today. You're going to be in two groups. The first group that plays the front nine, I'll be with you. John will be with the second group. Then we will switch. John will be with the first group and I'll join the second group." The look on the men's faces was priceless.

"I know it sounds confusing but the main point is that I will get an opportunity to watch and critique everyone. Are there any questions?"

Stuart looked at the men but no one said anything. He then walked onto the first tee. He motioned everyone to join him.

"There are four different colored tees. Since you all are beginners, I want everyone to tee off from the white tee." Before the men teed off, Stuart had them look at the fairway from behind the white tee.

"The course's fairway is expansive, fairly wide, and straight. I suggest you try and hit the ball as straight as possible. In doing so, I assure you that you will be able to reach the green without having to worry about the tall grass to the right and left, the trees, and sand traps."

Although Stuart kept asking if anyone had any questions, not one of them asked a single question. He could tell they were anxious to get started.

"Gentlemen, I don't want you worrying about the score. John and I will keep it. What I want you to do is to concentrate on the game, the course, and to keep the pace of play moving along."

With emphasis, Stuart gave the men last minute instructions. "Remember to keep your head down. Keep your eye on the ball, don't try to kill the ball, and take a full swing. Remember that you're not going to hit a perfect shot every time. Most of all—have fun."

Over all, the men did a good job of keeping up the pace of golf play. When the men were golfing, they were surprised at how supportive and complimentary Stuart and John had been—they did not fail to comment when one of them did something right—making the right club selection, swinging the club correctly, hitting the ball straight, or making a good putt. The first group did not have to wait long before the second group finished their golf round. Motioning everyone to gather around, Stuart began.

"Gentlemen, I hope you enjoyed your lessons as well as your first round of golf." Then he let out a low snicker. The men looked at each other and shrugged their shoulders, not understanding the humor of what Stuart said.

"There is no way that anyone can prepare any new golfer for their first round of golf. I just hope you were not too hard on yourself. For the most part you all did a good job of remembering what to do and what not to do. Golf is not an easy sport. It's challenging both mentally and physically."

With seriousness in his voice he continued. "Rather than take more lessons, I suggest you get out there and golf as much as possible. After several months of golfing then you might want to take additional lessons. By golfing often, you'll begin to get a better understanding of the game."

Digging into a sports bag, Stuart pulled out a handful of envelopes.

"Since this is our last lesson together, I wanted to give each of you something that might help your golf game."

Looking at the envelopes, Stuart began calling each man's name. While giving out the envelopes, he asked that no one open them until he had passed them all out.

"You can now open the envelope." Watching each man's face, Stuart explained that he had made up a "critique card" for each man.

"As you can see, the critique card is similar to a report card. The card not only critiques your golf lessons but it includes how well you golfed today, along with your score for the round."

The men let out loud moans and groans. Stuart held up his hand. "Please don't take the grades or your score too seriously. The grades were used only so you could gauge how well you're doing in a particular area. If it makes you feel any better, no one got an "A." In fact, I couldn't get an "A" in certain areas."

Each of the men was appreciative of Stuart taking the time to give them a critique of their golfing and said as much. When Woody looked at Donnie, he could have sworn his eyes were wet.

"Look, I know today was a little overwhelming. It's hard to remember everything you need to do when golfing. As I stated earlier, everyone did a good job for first-time golfers." Stuart hoped they believed him because it was true.

"That's it guys. I wish you all well, good luck, and you've been a great class. Remember, have fun!"

After golfing, the men found themselves back at Perkins. Everyone agreed that golfing on an actual course was nothing like hitting the ball on the golf range. Both groups of men compared notes. From their stories, they were all hitting golf balls to the right or to the left, in the bushes, in the trees, in the sand traps, and they all hit at least one ball in the water, except for Billy Ray. He managed to hit the ball over the water on his first try.

The men were taken back when even Lenny and Billy Ray who hit the ball consistently straight on the golf range had problems on the golf course. Lenny and Billy Ray had a problem in choosing the right club to hit. As a result, they hit the ball too far, which sent the ball off the green, or they hit the ball way too short. The men said Lenny did have a couple of impressive shots on the par 3 holes. He managed to get on the green with his first hit off the tee but unfortunately he could not putt the ball anywhere near the hole.

"Does anyone plan on taking more lessons?" Lenny asked.

No one answered.

Finally, Woody spoke up. "I think I'll take Stuart's advice. I'll golf some and then decide whether I want to take more lessons. What about you?"

"Well, I was thinking, how do you feel about golfing Sunday mornings?" Quickly Lenny moved on.

"I was thinking we could golf on Sundays and golf at different courses. Our Sunday golf would replace our golf lesson. We would be practicing on the golf courses and honing our skills. What do you think?"

Regretfully, Lenny lost his excitement. He thought the men would have been more enthusiastic about golfing on Sundays. Instead they sat saying nothing. He was sorry he brought it up.

At last Austin said he would have to check with his wife. As Lenny looked around the table everyone joined in and basically said the same thing.

"What about you?" Lenny looked at Donnie.

"I need to check with Raymond, my significant other."

Woody called himself mumbling under his breath but everyone heard what he said, "No different than having a wife."

"Please Woody don't go there. That was uncalled for." Immediately, Russell made the comment before things got out of hand. Everyone was pleasantly surprised that Russell stood up for Donnie.

Playing innocent, Woody flew up his hands defensively. "What did I say wrong?"

No one commented as they turned their attention back to Lenny.

"I tell you what, I'll call Stuart and ask him to recommend some golf courses. You all can call me and let me know what you want to do."

"For those that want to golf great and those that don't want to golf or are unable to golf that's cool too. Once I know who's all golfing, I'll make all the arrangements regarding the golf courses, the directions, cost, and tee times."

CHAPTER 31

When Austin answered the phone, he heard his youngest sister's voice. Instead of her saying hello, she sprayed him with some colorful words that a lady should not use. At first, he had no idea what she was talking about and then it hit him. He had given her telephone number to Lenny and he forgot to mention it to her. It was an honest mistake. He really thought Ebony was going to tell her about Lenny since it was her idea. He let Eloise rant and rave until he was able to get a word in.

"Eloise, please calm down."

He did not want to further fuel her anger so he tried to apologize. "I'm sorry. I only gave him your telephone number and…"

Eloise blasted him before he could finish his sentence. "But you didn't ask me first."

"I know and again I apologize." Austin wanted to shift the blame on someone else.

"Look, if you want to be mad at someone, call your sister Ebony. She's the one who asked me to give Lenny your number."

"Don't worry I plan on calling Miss Ebony and telling her what I think about her idea. Do you two think I'm that pitiful that I can't find my own man?"

Calmly, Austin answered, "no."

"I think Ebony..." Again, he tried shifting the fault on Ebony but it did not work.

"If that's not what you thought then you should have told Ebony to mind her own business. You don't see me all up into your business, do you?" She snapped.

Eloise did not wait for an answer from Austin. Without any further discussion, she slammed the phone down.

Listening to the dial tone for a second, he finally hung up. Although he did not get an opportunity to answer her, she was right. He should never have let Ebony talk him into giving Eloise's telephone number to Lenny. He punched in Eloise's phone number and changed his mind. He decided that it would probably be better to wait a few days. By then, she would have cooled down. He loved his sister and he did not like it when she was mad at him.

Eloise was livid at Austin for giving her number to that man and even madder at Ebony for asking him to do it. She could not believe Austin had given her telephone number to a complete stranger without consulting her first. At the moment Eloise was not interested in dating him or any man. Most of the men she had dated were no good, lying, cheating, nonworking, good for nothing, womanizers. Recently, all the men she had dated were a waste of her time. Some day she would love to meet a man that she could love and he would love her.

The last long-term relationship she was in, the man shattered her heart. When Eloise thought about it, she knew he was too good to be true. He was handsome, had a decent paying job, drove a new car, lived alone, was kind, considerate, and had manners. Well, the man was less than truthful about his availability. When she met him, he was already engaged but he had failed to share that information with her.

Instead, as fate would have it, Eloise found out unexpectedly. As she was walking past the office bulletin board, she noticed a wedding announcement. Shocked, she could not believe what she was reading. The man she had been dating was marrying a woman who worked with her—only in a different department. In addition, the office was giving the woman a bridal shower.

When Eloise confronted him about his up coming wedding, he denied it at first. He stated that there was some mistake. It wasn't him. Finally, he admitted it. His excuse for not mentioning his engagement was because he was not sure he was ready to make a commitment like marriage. With the wedding only two weeks away, he told Eloise that he still had options.

Eloise had heard enough. She told him that if he did not start telling women that he was about to get married, she would tell his fiancé about them. In addition, she would be watching him after he got married. If she saw or heard anything about him talking to any woman other than his wife, he would have a price to pay and he would not like the cost.

For the moment, she was a happy, independent black woman who did not need a man to make her life complete. To occupy her time she volunteered as a mentor for high school girls. When she was not mentoring she was busy with her fixer-upper house she had bought.

Eloise decided that when or if Mr. Harper called she would be polite but she would let him know that she had so many obligations that at the moment she did not have much time for dating. As she thought about some other reasons why she could not go out with him, the ringing telephone broke into her concentration.

CHAPTER 32

Ring . . . Ring…Ring.

"Hello, may I please speak to Miss Eloise Hayes."

Another telemarketer, Eloise thought. She went into attack mode.

"This is Eloise Hayes. Before you start your prepared spill about whatever product you're selling, let me inform you that this call may be monitored and recorded. Now you may continue."

"I'm sorry. I'm not selling anything. I have been taking golf lessons with your brother Austin. He gave me your telephone number. He said you knew I would be calling."

Eloise could not believe she had done that. This man was going to think she was a raving lunatic. But she hated telemarketers. As a result, she had a variety of tactics for when they called. She must have taken too long to answer because she heard him say something about hanging up.

"No, no. I owe you an apology." She thought she better explain.

"I get so many calls from telemarketers that I have come up with a number of strategies to deal with them, hoping they'll put me on their don't call list."

"I see," Lenny responded slowly.

From the sound of his voice, Eloise could only imagine what he must be thinking. She wouldn't blame him if he hung up and threw her telephone number away.

"Let's start over again. Hi, I'm Eloise Hayes."

"Hi, I'm Lenny Harper." He waited to see if she had anything else to say. Hearing nothing, he moved on.

"I hope you didn't mind your brother giving me your number?"

Eloise did not answer him because she did not like the fact that her brother had not consulted her before he gave him her number. Rather than say anything she would regret, she said nothing.

"I'm not sure how much your brother told you about me."

"Actually he said very little about you. What do you do for a living?"

Talk about cutting through the chase. She wasted no time wanting to know if he had a job and if so what was his career field. She was no different than other professional women who did not want to date blue-collar brothers. As a result his answer was terse.

"I work for the transit authority."

He stopped and when he continued he sounded apologetic. "I drive the city bus."

"You don't have to apologize for doing honest work. My Father retired from the postal service. He carried that mail bag for thirty years."

Lenny had not meant his response to sound like an apology but he had been so tired of sisters blowing him off because he was a blue-collar worker. After hearing about her father, he felt like a jerk.

Well, at least she was cool with the fact that he was not a college graduate. He had gone to college but he had not finished. It was his sophomore year when he dropped out. His mother had been diagnosed with breast cancer, resulting in him having to quit college. In order to support his mother and two younger sisters, he applied for the highest paying jobs he could get without a degree and those jobs were being a police officer, bus driver, or a fireman. The transit authority was the first to offer him a job and he took it. His mother recovered from cancer, his two sisters were out of high school, he had gotten married, bought a house, and he had been working for the transit authority for ten years. At that point he never thought about going back to college to get a degree.

"What do you do for a living?"

"I'm an accountant."

"How do you like being an accountant?"

"It pays the bills. My real passion is clothes. One day I hope to open my own boutique."

Although the beginning of their conversation started off rocky, they ended up talking for about an hour and a half. Lenny and Eloise commented on how long they had been talking. Lenny could not believe he had talked to her that long because he hated talking on the phone. Eloise was surprised that she actually liked hearing what Lenny had to say.

Unlike most of the women he had been married to and had dated, he and Eloise actually had some commonalities. They had just skimmed the surface, but they liked to bowl, loved college football and basketball, and enjoyed reading murder mysteries.

After several weeks, Lenny realized that his pity party had finally ended. He was no longer thinking about Mandy. He knew he was on the rebound and he needed to take it slow, but he was beginning to have feelings for Eloise.

Every time he talked to Eloise on the telephone, he was in awe as to how much he enjoyed her conversation. He could not remember the last time, including Mandy, when a woman had kept him interested enough that their relationship was more than just being in the bedroom.

Eloise was intelligent, sincere, thoughtful, and she made him laugh. On top of all of that, she was attractive and she had no children. He knew what his flaws were—but he wondered what could possibly be wrong with her?

Their telephone calls finally led to dating. After dating Eloise for several weeks, Lenny decided that he liked her enough that he could probably fall in love with her. She was full of surprises and she was the one who wanted to take their relationship to another level. It was not that he did not want to make love to her but somehow Eloise was different. If they were going to go to the next level in their relationship then he wanted to be sure that they were going to be committed to each other.

There was not a minute that went by when he was not thinking about her. There were times when he had to admonish himself about calling her. Talking to her was the highlight of his day. Therefore, he wanted to share everything with her. He hated to say it but his nose was so wide open that a large semi-truck could drive through it. Unless he was reading Eloise wrong, he sensed that his feelings were not one sided.

When Austin asked how things were going between him and his sister, Lenny was vague. He did not want to feel any pressure regarding his relationship with his sister. He knew Eloise well enough now to know that she wanted to keep their relationship private. So Lenny doubted that she had shared anything with Austin about how much they had been seeing one another.

Lenny wanted to be truthful with Eloise about everything in his life. He knew he would be taking a risk but he felt as though he could be open and honest with her.

"Eloise, I don't want any secrets between us. I don't need to know every aspect of your past and vice versa but there is one thing you need to know about me."

Eloise had been waiting. She knew Lenny was too good for words. Up until now, she thought she had been dreaming. He was not the perfect man but he did have qualities that she had been looking for in a man—attractive, thoughtful, caring, funny, and loving. She could not remember a time when she had felt so secure in a man's arms and he did not want anything from her. She waited.

"After my last divorce, I guess I was lonely or looking for love in all the wrong places or something. Anyway, I had an affair with a married woman." Lenny's voice had lowered when he finished the part about the woman being married. Watching Eloise's face, he saw signs of disgust, anger, and then she made an unexpected comment. "Why do men have to do that? So typical of a man to break one of the "big ten."

Because she was talking under her breath Lenny could not understand exactly what she had said but he thought she said something about him breaking one of the Ten Commandments. Then shockingly she made herself clear as she looked sternly at him.

"Look, I'm not going to judge you and let me make this clear—I certainly don't approve of the fact that you participated in an indiscreet manner that caused a married woman to break her vows."

She paused for a moment. Lenny felt beads of sweat forming on his forehead.

"However, I appreciate you being honest with me and I find it refreshing."

Lenny did not know what to say. He was just happy that she was not going to stop seeing him because of his indiscretion.

After Lenny had discussed that matter with Eloise, he knew she was the one. When he met Mandy, he was sure she was his *"soul mate"* but now that he had gotten to know Eloise, he knew that what he had felt for Mandy was not love. In fact, Lenny had been married three times, had dated many women, but this was the first time he could say that he knew what love was and that he was in love.

CHAPTER 33

Russell wanted to golf on Sundays but he knew that without Connie saying he could, it was hopeless. Deep down inside, he knew what her answer was going to be.

"Your lessons are over," Connie screamed.

Russell did something he never did. He screamed back. "I know the lessons are over but the instructor said we needed to golf as much as possible if we were going to improve our game. It was suggested that in order to practice, the men from the class should continue golfing on Sunday mornings."

Russell had stretched the truth a little. Regardless of how much he wanted to golf on Sundays, he had to be careful because Connie might call Stuart to see whether he recommended that the men continue to golf.

Later, he knew Connie would find a way to punish him for raising his voice at her. He did not care. When he was golfing, he felt free of her. Some of the men had been judgmental when he told them about Connie but they had come around and had actually been supportive. For the first time in a long time, he was meeting men and when he thought about it, yes, even making some friends.

Russell had lowered his voice to a calming tone. "You even told me that you had to practice to get better."

Softening her voice Connie countered. "Look. It's not that I don't want you to golf with these men but…"

Thinking about Russell golfing, she wondered what harm would it be if he started golfing on Sunday? What was really bothering her? She knew—she did not know these men. She needed to meet them but she had not figured out a way to do it.

Patiently, Russell waited for his wife to give him permission to golf on Sunday mornings. As much as he wanted to continue going to Perkins with the guys, he would be happy just to golf with them. Maybe, in time, he could join them after they golfed, but for now he had to take one step at a time.

Finally Connie consented. "Fine. You can golf. However, only on Sunday mornings."

To Russell's surprise, Connie went even further with her permission. "I have an idea, why don't you continue going to Perkins with the men after you golf?"

Looking at Connie, Russell wondered what was going on inside her head. He was pleased with Connie's decision but then he waited for her to drop the bomb. He knew one was coming.

For several minutes Russell waited to see if she had anything else to say. Since she seemed to be finished with him, he turned away from her and headed to his home office. He had some unfinished transcribing to do. Taking only a few steps, Russell heard Connie add sweetly but insincerely.

"Perhaps one Sunday, I could golf with you. We could also ask two of the men to join us. That way, I could get to meet some of your new male friends."

Russell was unresponsive. So that was it. Connie wanted to meet some of the guys. He merely smiled. If he could help it, she would never meet any of them.

CHAPTER 34

It was time that Bob told Nessa that he was going to golf on Sundays. He knew she would be angry but he had made his decision. There was no need in postponing what he had to do.

"Why do you have to golf on Sundays?"

"What difference does it make? I was taking lessons on Sunday mornings."

"I know but that's the point. You were taking lessons. The lessons are over. Why not pick another day."

"What day would that be? I only have the weekends, so don't say Saturdays?"

Vanessa did not answer her husband right away. She cautioned herself about being overly possessive.

"I don't know. It seems as though you and I could golf on Sundays."

"In the future, we will golf together, even Sundays, but right now I need to golf with someone on my level. I don't want to…"

Stopping his sentence Bob looked at his wife. He did not want instructions from her when he was golfing. He wanted to get better at the game before they golfed together. Why couldn't she understand that?

Silence took up all the space in the room. Vanessa and Bob were not looking at each other. Suggesting that Bob learn how to golf, Vanessa never thought it would develop into an argument every time the subject of golf was brought up. Or was it her? Was she turning the subject of golf into an unnecessary disagreement?

Without further discussion, Bob dialed Lenny's number. He knew from the look on Nessa face, she was not pleased as she watched and listened to him talk to Lenny.

He had made up his mind. The main reason she was upset was because they could not golf together. He recalled Nessa's response when he first hinted at the idea of golfing on Sundays. It still rang in his head.

"Bob, I don't understand why we can't golf together. Since I golf, I could help you improve your game. You really need to golf with someone experienced. You would be surprised at what I could show you. Besides the only thing you can learn from people who can barely golf themselves are bad habits."

From that conversation, he knew that golfing on Sundays was going to be an uphill battle. Perhaps he should have compromised but he did not want to. He thought she would have been happy that he was spending more time with some men. But no, if he was not spending time with her then it was a problem.

As it was, they worked together, ate together, and played together. The Sunday golfing was the only time he was not with her. Besides, he knew in a very short time, they would be golfing together. So for now, he was going to golf with the guys on Sundays.

CHAPTER 35

"Raymond, do you mind if I golf on Sundays with the guys?"

"I don't care but I can't believe you want to golf with these men. You're the one who said they're not comfortable with you being gay."

"That's not totally true." Thinking before he continued.

"To be honest, there's only one guy who is really uptight about me being gay and that's old Woody."

"You mean the other guys are cool with it?" Donnie had hesitated a little too long with his response. Raymond made his point.

"See what I mean? If you have to think about it then they aren't all that cool with it. I've made my case."

"That's not why I hesitated. I was just thinking that when I told the men I was gay, they were cool with it. I'm telling you Raymond, Woody was the only one who I would say is really homophobic."

Donnie thought about all the guys and they were okay with his sexuality. In fact, since they had the one conversation about him being gay, to his surprise, no one had treated him any differently. Everyone continued to think of him as they did before he admitted that he was gay. Smiling, Donnie thought about Woody who had a tendency to make dumb ass comments, from time to time, but that was Woody.

"Well are the men okay with your gayness or not?"

"I think so. I mean when I think about Woody. He's from a different generation. I bet if I talked to him about what he prefers to be called—Negro, African American, or black—he would probably answer colored." Donnie laughed but Raymond stood stone faced.

"Look, Woody, is old school—a flash in the past. It's not just about gays that he has hang-up's about…" Raymond cut him off in mid-sentence.

"Why is this so important to you?"

"To be honest, this is the first time I actually feel as though I have connected with straight men. I'm not hiding my sexuality and they aren't judging me or treating me like I have some sort of disease."

"Are you sure that's the reason and the only reason?"

Donnie wished Raymond would leave him alone. That was the only reason why he wanted to continue golfing with these men. He liked golf, wanted to get better at it, and he liked the friends he had made.

"Yes. I'm sure. The men don't care about my sexual orientation. When we are golfing, everyone gets the same treatment. Golfing is like any other sport—the only thing men care about is whether you can play or not."

"And you're willing to cope with Woody?"

"Woody's harmless."

"I still don't get it but it's your Sundays. If you want to spend time with these men, then go for it. Just don't ask me to join you. But then again, wouldn't that be a hoot!" They laughed.

The image of Woody's reaction to Donnie suggesting that Raymond join them in a round of golf made him laugh even harder. Donnie thought Woody would probably act similar to how some whites act when blacks move into an all white neighborhood.

CHAPTER 36

"I thought you didn't want to golf with these men?"

"I never said that."

"Well, I thought you didn't want to golf with them especially when you found out that one of the men was gay."

"Yeah, I was upset about that but he doesn't have to golf in my foursome. I mean over all I enjoy being with the men. In addition, you're the one who was harping about me needing to do something with my time. And now…" His voice faded off.

"Oh no. I don't care if you golf on Sundays. I was just making a point."

Amanda was actually very pleased that Woody wanted to golf on Sundays. This was the first time in a long time that she had seen Woody so energetic about anything or anybody. She would like to meet these men. Amanda had an idea.

"Woody I would love to invite all the men and their wives or significant others over for a Sunday brunch."

"I don't know." Woody was shaking his head.

"Why not?"

"Because we have a routine. We are in the habit of going to

Perkins and having…"

"Come on Woody. We're only talking about one Sunday. At least ask them. Please, for me."

Woody thought about the brunch as well as the men and their golfing. Admittedly, he had not wanted to learn to golf but now he was not only enjoying golf but also the after golf outing at Perkins.

By and large, the conversations were lively and at times, controversial but mostly just good-natured men talk. The type of talk you used to be able to have at a barbershop. But with so many of the barbershops having women barbers and women getting services in a barbershop, they just aren't the same.

"Woody?" Caught up in his thoughts he had forgotten about Amanda and the brunch until he heard her voice.

"I'm sorry. What were you saying?"

"Will you ask them?"

"Okay." Reluctantly he told his wife that he would ask the guys about coming to their house for brunch.

"Don't forget. It's for them and their significant others."

"I won't forget."

What worried Woody about having guests in their home was that he was never sure which Amanda would show up. He had to admit that the past several weeks had been an improvement. Her mood swings were not as bad as they had been but he still worried about her temperament. He was accustomed to her rudeness and not talking to him. However, when you invite people into your home you have to put yourself out there and be hospitable from the time they arrive and until they leave. He was concerned that the brunch might be too stressful for her.

CHAPTER 37

Billy Ray and Ebony were having dinner with Austin and Jessica. They could not believe that the Outback Restaurant was not crowded. But then they reminded themselves that they had arrived just as Outback was opening their doors for dinner at four o'clock.

"Now that the golf lessons are over, are you all ready to golf with us?" Jessica asked.

Billy Ray and Austin did not respond. Austin tried changing the subject but Jessica persisted.

"What are you all going to do about golf since your lessons are over?"

Hesitating, Austin finally told their wives that the guys wanted to continue golfing on Sundays. Since the lessons were over, the instructor suggested that they golf as much as possible. Austin and Billy Ray were prepared to defend why they should golf on Sundays but Jessica and Ebony agreed without any persuasion.

Ebony said, "In fact, I think it's better to golf with someone on your level rather than golf with someone who's been golfing for years. Golf can be frustrating and humbling." Pausing, Ebony smiled as she thought about golf.

She continued, "You'll find that you'll have these shining moments such as when you hit the ball off the tee and it goes straight, or you hit the ball off the tee and it goes on the green giving you an opportunity to make birdie or par." Ebony paused for a moment to see if Billy Ray and Austin were grasping the point she was trying to make.

"What I'm trying to say is that these shining moments will draw you back out on the golf course so you can see if you can do it again. I know I'm speaking for me and Jessica when I say that we're glad you guys have agreed to continue golfing together. You can support and encourage each other."

Ebony was curious as she asked, "Austin I haven't had time to talk to you. What's going on with Eloise and what's his name?"

"Don't ask me," Austin answered in a huffy voice.

"First of all, I wouldn't dare ask her about Lenny. Not the way she cursed me out about giving her number to him. Besides, do you remember what I told you?"

Ebony nodded. She felt badly that Eloise had gotten so mad at Austin because it had been her idea.

"If you must know Miss Nosy, I did give Lenny the number and he called her but beyond that I know nothing. I sort of asked him about Eloise and he shrugged it off, like it was none of my business—you know Eloise style. I figured that was my clue to keep my nose out of it and I suggest you do the same."

"Come on Austin. I can't believe you don't' want to know what's going on."

"I don't. Billy Ray, you better talk to your wife. I'm serious. When I say I don't want to know about Eloise's love life, I'm not joking. Ebony, I know you haven't forgotten when I hooked her up with Ray Johnson?" Ebony tried to suppress her laughter but she couldn't.

"See you think that was funny. The man still doesn't speak to me." Before they could continue discussing Eloise, the waiter was standing at the table.

Taking their orders and before leaving the table, the waiter asked,

"Will this be one check or two separate checks?"

In unison they answered, "two separate checks."

"Who's with whom?" The waiter asked as he looked around the table.

Shocked Billy Ray could barely believe it. The four of them go to restaurants at least twice a week, but this was a first. In three years, this waiter was the only one who did not assume that Jessica was Billy Ray's wife and that Ebony was Austin's wife.

The expression on Billy Ray's face was precious. Billy Ray reminded Ebony of what youngsters look like when they are surprised because they actually received the toy or whatever they asked for at Christmas or for their birthday.

"Are you okay Billy Ray? I know you're in shock, but say something."

"You're right. I'm completely speechless and pleasantly surprised. I am going to give that boy the biggest tip he's probably had in a long time and he won't even know why." Hysterically, they laughed.

CHAPTER 38

When Justin finally went to church with Suzanne, you would have thought they had hit the lottery. He had no idea that him attending church was going to make Suzanne feel as though she was on cloud nine.

Two Sundays in a row, he had attended church and now he had to break the news to her that he was going to be golfing again on Sunday mornings. The compromise would be that he would attend the Sunday evening service.

To help him, as well as their marriage, he needed to golf on Sundays. The camaraderie of the men on Sunday mornings was the catalyst that was helping him make some decisions about his life that would affect him and Suzanne's future. After dinner, Justin decided he would tell Suzanne.

"Honey. We need to talk."

"Yes, we do."

Justin was taken off guard. He didn't expect that Suzanne had anything to discuss even though she had been preoccupied lately. He wondered what she wanted to discuss.

"What about after dinner?" asked Suzanne.

Suzanne had been putting off telling Justin that she was pregnant but she was gaining weight and she could not hide the pregnancy much longer. She had no idea what he needed to tell her. Whatever it was, he seemed serious.

"That's what I was thinking. We seem to be on the same page."

After dinner and dessert they went out on the lanai to sit. They were silent as they gazed at the breath-taking sunset.

Suzanne broke the tranquility. "Why don't you go first Justin?"

"No. Ladies before gentlemen."

Nervously, they both laughed.

"Suzanne, are you okay? You seem a little edgy. What you want to tell me can't be that bad."

Folding her hands in her lap, Suzanne closed her eyes and silently prayed.

"Please God give me the strength I need to tell Justin about our baby."

"Okay, here it goes. Justin, you know I love you."

She did not require a response from him. She was trying to find the appropriate words to tell him about the baby.

"And I know you love me. I also know you don't want…"

"Wait, if this is about children. Let me explain myself. I don't think I did a very good job when we were discussing children." His tone was soft and he was holding Suzanne's hand.

"Some day, it would be nice to have children. It's just that we haven't been married that long. I'm trying to adjust to life outside of prison and you're trying to adjust to having a husband. I would also like to find another job. I don't think that now is a good time to start a family."

"Well sometimes, God makes decisions that are taken out of our…"

"Are you trying to tell me that you're pregnant?" His tone was harsh.

"I guess I am." Her response sounded more like a whimper.

"I can just imagine what your old man said."

Justin lost his temper as he jumped up. Justin did not wait to hear her answer as he lowered his voice trying to sound like her father.

"If it weren't for me, you and Justin wouldn't have a roof over your head. When no one else would hire him, I gave him a job. Now, I'm going to have to take care of my grandchild too."

Suzanne thought to herself but did not say to Justin that he was right about her daddy. He would never have chosen Justin to be her husband and his son-in-law. However, whatever thoughts and dislikes her daddy had regarding Justin, he had never spoken the words to her. After all, Suzanne was his only daughter and she knew her daddy loved her. Therefore, he would do anything for her, Justin, and yes his unborn grandchild. Suzanne swallowed hard, trying to keep the tears away. Her voice cracked.

"Daddy isn't like that. He's just trying to be helpful." Suzanne defended her father.

"What's wrong with that?"

"What's wrong?" In disbelief, Justin looked at her with resentment in his tone.

"You don't work for your daddy. You know and I know your old man thinks I'm nothing but a con artist, looking for a free ride. I don't care what I do. Your father has no respect for me. He thinks I'm nothing and I will never amount to nothing. Not to mention, he thinks I'm not good enough for you."

Suzanne felt the tears coming and she tried to hold them in. Her heart was racing and she could barely breathe. As she tried to speak, only a whisper acted as her voice. Before she could muster up a stronger voice to answer Justin's accusation, he had turned and gone into the house. He had left her, sitting alone. Her shoulders shook uncontrollably as she sobbed quietly.

Suzanne didn't know how long she had been crying but when the tears finally dried up, the evening sky had turned dark and the night temperature had caused her to shiver. Finding strength to stand up, she walked inside the house.

The house was not only dark but it also seemed empty. Where was Justin? If their marriage was going to survive, she and Justin were going to have to learn how to communicate better. He never did tell her…she heard a noise.

"Justin is that you?"

"Yes," he answered.

He was sitting in a chair in the dark. He felt so ashamed as to how he reacted to the news of his wife's pregnancy. He had lost his temper and acted badly. If he wanted his marriage to work, he was going to have to learn how to discuss issues with his wife. He was going to have to face the music rather than stomping off like a little boy who couldn't have his way.

His reaction had more to do with him being scared than anything. He was taking on too much too soon. He did not know how to be a father. There had been no male role models in his life when he was growing up. In addition, he wanted to get to know his wife better before they brought another person into their lives.

"Suzanne, please come here."

Justin pulled her onto his lap. Gently he caressed her and massaged her back.

"You know I love you and would do anything for you. I acted like an ungrateful, unfeeling, uncaring…" She shushed him.

"What I know is that God answers prayers. He will make a way for us. Just you wait and see. You have to have faith Justin. We're in this together, along with God."

Justin knew she was right but where was God when it seemed like the walls were coming down all around him. Tightly he hugged her and wanted her to know that he would be there for her and the baby. He was going to be a good father. He was going to be a part of a family—his family. Something he never had.

Maybe this would be the first step of stopping his family cycle of being in prison. As far back as he could remember most of the men in his family had gone to prison—uncles, cousins, his father and him. But he would do everything in his power to make sure that his child would never see the inside of a prison. As they sat quietly, he continued to rub her back. His hands felt soothing and Suzanne felt comfortable but then she remembered that Justin had something to tell her.

"What did you want to tell me?"

Suzanne pulled away slightly from his embrace as she looked up into Justin's eyes.

"This isn't the time."

"Justin, this time is as good as any. What is it?"

Taking a deep breath through his nose, he slowly let the air escape through his mouth.

"As you know, the golf lessons are over. The instructor…well, the guys…" He could not get the words out.

Suzanne helped him out. "You want to golf on Sunday mornings?"

Gushing excitedly, Justin tried to explain.

"The instructor said that if we were to improve our game, we needed to golf on a regular basis. I can't explain it to you but golfing and being with these guys…well, it has been good for me. Suzanne I promise I'll go to Sunday evening service."

"Listen Justin. I understand more than you know. Do what you need to do. I'll support your decision about Sunday golf."

"You are an angel. I don't deserve you. I love you so much."

Justin felt like the luckiest man in the world. He pulled his wife closer to him and gave her a long, deep kiss.

CHAPTER 39

The men took longer than Lenny expected to respond about golfing on Sundays. However, for Lenny there was no urgency because his Sundays had turned from boring to busy since he had met Eloise. He had mixed emotions about golfing on Sundays. He was looking forward to golfing again but yet he was miserable when he thought about not being able to spend his Sundays with Eloise.

When he told Eloise about the possibility of golfing on Sundays, she was more supportive than he expected. She said how could she not want him to golf on Sundays when she was an avid golfer. As far as she was concerned, it was perfect because they would have just one more thing in common. Plus, she could not wait until they could golf together.

When Lenny called Stuart, he was more than eager to give him a list of recommended golf courses.

"To start you off, I suggest you try to get tee times at Orange Blossom in The Villages, The Links at Spruce Creek South, Lakes of Lady Lake in Lady Lake, and Silver Lake in Leesburg."

"Thanks, Stuart."

"No problem, and tell the fellows I said, hello and to have fun."

Stuart had selected these golf courses because he considered them to be easy for first time golfers but yet challenging. He had called the courses, *"Golf Friendly."* As far as Lenny was concerned, if the courses were anything like Baseline, then he did not understand the word "friendly."

Lenny had received nothing but positive responses from the men. Everyone was excited and could not wait until they golfed again. To Lenny's surprise, Russell would be joining them.

The first golf course they golfed at was the Silver Lake Golf Course in Leesburg. The course provided the men with a different type of challenge. There was one hole where everyone had to hit the ball over the water. There was no drop area. After each man lost three golf balls a piece, each of them finally managed to hit the ball over the water. They all enjoyed their round of golf, but they all agreed that golfing could be exhausting and definitely overwhelming.

The one shining moment of the day was on the last hole. The first group had finished their round and was waiting for the second group to finish. Suddenly, the waiting group heard loud shouts and cheers. When the second group approached the clubhouse, they shouted that Russell had made a par, the only par between the two groups. Since it was the first par made by any of the men, Russell's reward was that he got to keep the scorecard.

To keep the celebration going, the men went to Perkins as usual. As a further treat, the men told Russell that they would buy his meal since he was the first one to make a par. The men were more boisterous than usual and there were plenty of stories and laughs regarding their round of golf.

During the talking and laughter, Woody had made several attempts to get the men's attention. Picking up a knife, he used it to hit the side of a glass. The sound was loud enough which caused the men to stop talking. Before the discussions could begin again,

Woody quickly took advantage of the quietness.

"Don't shoot the messenger but my wife put me up to this. One Sunday, instead of us meeting at Perkins when we finish our round of golf, my wife and I would like to invite you and your better halves to our house for a Sunday Brunch. Oh, and Lenny, you can bring someone if you like." To Woody's astonishment, no one said anything, not even Lenny.

It was Russell who finally responded to Woody. "I think I'm the only one who has children. I'm not sure it would be a good idea for them to be at an all adult gathering."

Quickly Russell added, "But I'll ask my wife and see if we can attend."

After Russell stopped speaking all the other men began to say they had to discuss it with their wives.

Donnie didn't say anything. For some reason he wanted Woody to invite him personally. Then he would feel as though the invitation was genuine. In addition, he expected Woody to say that his significant other was also invited—just like the invitation he extended to Lenny.

Wonders never cease, Woody did just what Donnie wanted and without anyone prompting him. He knew that it took a lot for Woody to invite him and Raymond to the brunch. He appreciated it more than Woody would ever know. Donnie was thrilled about the invitation and he could not wait to tell Raymond.

The morning had gone way to fast. All the men felt they could have stayed and talked longer, especially about golfing at Silver Lake. For some reason, golfing at Silver Lake seemed more action-packed and exciting than golfing at Baseline. Everyone thought it was because they golfed independent of their instructor. It made them feel like they were real golfers. Russell said that it reminded him of the first time he drove his father's car by himself.

Every Sunday that the men golfed at one of the courses, they seemed to have more fun than the last. They found the golf courses to be different and each course had its own unique challenge. Each Sunday, the men could see that their golfing was improving. More of the men were making pars and Lenny made the first birdie. However, all the men found that as quickly as they could do something right on one hole, they were just as able to do everything wrong on the next hole. As a result, they all learned lessons in humility.

Each of the men had to admit that their outings to Perkins had caused the men to forge friendships that might not have happened if they had not started their after golf outings. Each Sunday, the men were feeling more and more comfortable about sharing information about themselves and their personal lives.

Consulting their wives and significant others about the brunch, all the men thought it was a great way for everyone to get acquainted. The date had been set and the men canceled golf on that particular Sunday. The men agreed that it would be a long day and too tiring to golf, go home, shower and change clothes, and then go to Woody's house for a brunch.

Just before the men left Perkins, Woody reminded the men about the brunch. When Amanda first mentioned the brunch to Woody, he was apprehensive but now he was excited about having the men over. The men were walking to their cars when Woody remembered that they did not have directions to his house. He yelled to get their attention.

"Fellows, if you all could wait a minute. I have flyers with directions to my house."

As Woody passed out the flyers, he emphasized. "The Villages have gates at every entrance. All you have to do is push the button at the gate. The gate will lift up, giving you access inside The Villages."

CHAPTER 40

Woody lived in The Villages off 27/441, west of Orlando, Florida. The Villages was a retirement community for people 55 and over. Driving to The Villages, a person could not miss the billboards that stated, *"The Villages is the friendliest hometown."*

Russell and Connie left early so they could take a quick drive through The Villages. Although they did not live far from The Villages, they had never been there. They had heard so much about the retirement community that they wanted to take a quick tour. They stopped by the sales office and got a map and a brochure. When they were driving through The Villages, Russell commented about how beautiful it was. To Russell's surprise, Connie was complimentary and seemed impressed.

"Not only that, the landscaping is beautiful and it's so clean. Did you see all the golf cart traffic?"

"I did. Did you have a chance to look at the brochure?"

"Not really but listen to this Russell." There was excitement in Connie's voice.

"Nightly, The Villages has a variety of *"free"* entertainment such as a concert in the Church on Town Square, a live band, or a Disc

Jockey. In addition, there are two bowling centers, two town squares, two movie theaters, a learning college, a boardwalk, a newspaper, radio and television stations, a hospital, swimming pools, recreation centers, a variety of shopping, and an array of restaurants. You're not going to believe this."

"What?"

"People from the surrounding communities are welcomed to enjoy the *"free"* entertainment."

"Wow. The Villages seems more like a resort or being on a cruise than a retirement community. What about golfing?"

"Let's see." Flipping through the brochure, Connie found it.

"It says that the residents golf *"free"* on the 9 hole golf courses. They have 16 of them and they pay to play the five, 18-hole golf courses."

"This place seems to have it all. Maybe this would be a nice community for us to think about when we retire?

"Oh, I'm impressed but I wouldn't want to live here. There's too many people, activity, and the traffic is probably horrendous." Connie snorted.

Russell could not believe what she was saying. Just a few minutes ago, she was going on about The Villages and now she would not consider living here. He wanted to suggest that they come back another time and bring the kids but after that comment, he decided not to. As Russell turned on to Woody's street, the houses were beautiful. Slowing the car to a snail's pace, Russell asked for the address.

"It's 3907. It's the beige house on the left."

As Russell parked in front of Woody's house, he pointed out to Connie the unusual landscaping. There was an assortment of different palm trees with lots of flowering bushes and flowers to compliment the greenery. Your eyes could not miss the display of different color hues. Standing admiring the landscaping, Russell looked around.

Connie commented, "I don't see any other cars, we might be the first ones to have arrived."

Russell rang the doorbell. Woody opened the door with a warm greeting.

"Welcome Russell." They shook hands.

"Hi Woody. This is my wife, Connie."

"I'm so glad to meet you." He extended his hand to Connie but she did not return the pleasantry.

"Where are your children?"

"Connie..." Russell corrected himself.

"We decided to get a babysitter."

"Well, you certainly could have brought them. In fact, we were looking forward to having them. I know Amanda will be disappointed that they didn't come. Please come in."

Amanda was on the lanai, which extended from one end of the house to the other. It was breath taking. Part of the lanai was enclosed with acrylic windows. An in-ground hot tub and a waterfall were strategically placed in the corner of the lanai that was screened covered. The enclosed part of the lanai had a built-in wet bar, grill, and counter. Tables and chairs, lounge chairs, a television, stereo, and plants filled the rest of the lanai. Under Connie's breath she grunted.

"So, this is how the rich and the famous live? I'm surprised there's no pool."

Russell shot her a stunned look. He hoped that Woody did not hear what she had said.

"Amanda, this is Russell and his wife Connie. They didn't bring the children. They left them at home with a sitter."

"Hi and welcome. I'm so glad you were able to come. I hope you know you could have brought the children. Please have a seat."

"We appreciate the invitation but we thought it was best to leave them at home. After all, they would have been the only children." Connie's response was terse and to the point.

With the slight reflection but noticeable change in her voice, she warned without stating it that she was no longer interested in discussing the whys of not bringing her children to the brunch. As she changed the subject, Russell looked at her with worried eyes.

"What a beautiful house you have. As Russell and I stood outside your house we were admiring your landscaping."

Russell hoped that Woody and Amanda did not notice that Connie's comment was phony and insincere. It was Amanda who responded to her compliment.

"Thank you Connie."

Woody could not stop looking at Russell's wife. Russell had mentioned that his wife had been a full-figured model before he met her. However, as Woody gazed at her, he could only visualize her as a female wrestler or Wonder Woman, as he looked at her bulging, well-defined arm and leg muscles. There was no mistake, Russell's wife worked out with weights on a regular basis. Woody guessed she could probably bench press at least 150-200 pounds.

Woody did not consider himself a wimp but this Amazon of a woman was intimidating and a force to be reckoned with. Just from her stares and manner of speech, she was making him quiver. When she spoke, she had a way of expressing herself so that her words were not only commanding but also demanding. Now that Woody had met Russell's wife in person, he could definitely see how she could beat Russell up, or any man for that matter.

"What can I get you two to drink?"

"We'll have something nonalcoholic to drink thank you."

"Tell me what you want. We have all kinds of soft drinks, unsweetened and sweet ice tea, and water."

As Russell made an attempt to respond, Connie put her hand on his knee as if to quiet him.

"I'll have a diet cola and Russell will have water with lemon."

Russell wished Connie would relax a little. Her behavior was making him uneasy. He prayed that nothing would upset her. In addition, Russell was nervous that one of the men might slip up and mention something he had told them about Connie or in jest make a reference to her beating him. When he thought about this brunch, he must have been out of his mind to bring her here.

Quickly the atmosphere had turned tense as Connie caught Woody staring at her. Connie returned Woody's stare with a piercing glare. Her eyes darted from Woody and then to Russell, looking for a clue. She wondered why he was looking at her so intently? She shook it off. Maybe, she was being paranoid and he was just admiring her beauty. After all, men still found her attractive.

    The doorbell rang. Woody was happy for the diversion. He chastised himself for looking a minute too long at Russell's wife. The look she gave him made the hairs on his arms stand up to attention. As Woody went to answer the door, he reminded himself not to spend much time alone talking to Mrs. Allen. She was far too intense for him.

CHAPTER 41

Answering the door, Woody welcomed Justin and his wife Suzanne. Just as Woody introduced them to everyone, the doorbell rang again.

Suzanne took a seat beside Connie. Russell had gone to use the bathroom.

"Hi, my name is Suzanne. Wasn't this thoughtful of Amanda to have the husbands and wives over so we all could meet one another? Not only that, this house is absolutely beautiful."

"I'm sure the cost matches the beauty of the house." Connie looked at Suzanne and made a face.

Suzanne thought Connie's comment was rude. She ignored it and said, "It was nice of Amanda to have us over, especially since the men seem to get along so well."

Abruptly Connie dismissed her small talk and took control of the subject. "Do you mind me asking what you do for a living...or do you work outside the home?"

"I don't mind you asking. I work outside the home. I'm a counselor for abused women." Suzanne noticed when she said, *"abused women"* Connie's demeanor altered a bit.

Before Suzanne could ask Connie about her career, she got up hastily from her seat. Without further acknowledging Suzanne, Connie walked into the house. Suzanne thought she mumbled something about going to find Russell.

At the same time Connie got up from her seat, Suzanne could not help but notice Justin and Amanda. She wondered what they could be talking about since she did not think Justin knew Woody's wife.

"You don't remember me do you?" Amanda looked at Justin but he did not look familiar to her.

Justin spoke in a low tone so others could not hear what he was saying. "You put me in prison."

Amanda's hand went to her throat. Her eyes darted around the room looking for Woody. Guardedly, she chose her words.

"I never put people in prison. The jury is responsible for coming up with the guilty or innocent verdict. Depending on the case and circumstances, the judge and or jury make the final decision about sentencing."

Watching Justin, he appeared angry to Amanda. She grew alarmed but then rejected away the fright. Why was she concerned? She was in her home with a room full of people.

Justin sensed the fear in Amanda's face. He hoped that he could convey to her that he was not there to harm her. Looking over his shoulder and around the bar, Justin made sure no one could hear him.

"Look, I did the crime and I did my time. I just wanted to ask you if you wouldn't say anything to anyone about me? None of the men know that I've been in prison."

Before Amanda could answer Justin, his wife appeared by his side. As a result, Amanda did not know whether to answer him or not. Amanda was sure his wife knew about his prison record but she did not want to cause him any unnecessary embarrassment.

When Suzanne had eased by Justin's side, he and Amanda's conversation came to a halt. From where he had been standing, Justin had kept his eye on Suzanne. As a result, he knew she had been watching the exchange of words he had been having with Amanda. Now that Suzanne was close enough to see Justin's face she was truly concerned. His facial expression let Suzanne know that he was not pleased with the conversation he had been having with Amanda.

Amanda gave Justin a nod in hope that he understood. She would not say anything. However, she would tell Woody as soon as all of their guests were gone.

"Amanda's a lawyer. She works for the DA's office. Amanda's the one who prosecuted me." Justin had whispered to Suzanne before she could ask what was wrong.

"So what?"

"So what?" His tone was annoyed as he spoke in a low abrasive tone.

"What you don't know is that none of the men know that I've been in prison for the past three years."

Momentarily Suzanne closed her eyes. She would never understand why Justin felt he had to hide the fact he had been in prison. True it was not something you just came right out and told people. However, once people got to know Justin, Suzanne saw no reason why he could not tell them.

"Come on Justin. It's not a big deal. I guess you want to leave?" Suzanne was equally annoyed and did not hide it in her voice.

Before Justin answered Suzanne, Woody walked in with Lenny and Eloise. Immediately Lenny approached Justin.

"Hey Justin." They shook hands.

"This can't be your wife because…" Lenny was about to say because she was so pretty but Justin bit his head off before he could finish his compliment.

"And why can't she be my wife? What I'm not good…"

Lightly tugging at Justin's elbow, Suzanne did not want Justin to say another word. He understood her message. Justin pursed his lips and said nothing further but looked fiercely at Lenny. Justin's temper had gotten the best of him and Suzanne wanted him to calm down. The man was joking with him. Turning and looking down at Suzanne, Justin glared irritably at her. Then he stomped off like a two-year-old child. He headed to a chair on the far end of the lanai.

Wanting to apologize to Lenny, Suzanne thought it would just make matters worse. Instead she followed behind Justin, embarrassed.

"Man, what did I say?"

"Nothing," answered Eloise.

"I wonder what that was all about?"

"I don't know but I don't think it had anything to do with what you were about to say about his wife."

CHAPTER 42

From behind, the woman who was standing at the bar looked familiar to Lenny but he was not sure. However, as she turned slowly around, his legs were wobbly. Trying to stop the shaking sensation, he put his hands in his pockets. His eyes had to be deceiving him. There had to be some mistake. Amanda Roberts, Woody's wife was "Mandy." His "Mandy."

Thinking and glancing around, Lenny wanted to escape. But he was trapped similar to an animal about to be caught. If this was a nightmare and he was dreaming, he wished he would wake up. Never in his wildest dreams would he have thought that Mandy was married to Woody.

"Lenny have you had a chance to meet my wife, Amanda?"

Lenny's mouth went dry and his heart was beating too fast. Clearing his throat, tripping over his tongue, and blowing air out his mouth, Lenny attempted to answer Woody but the words were stuck to his tongue.

Then with no forewarning Lenny felt water dripping down his back. Praying, Lenny hoped he was not visibly showing signs of perspiration anywhere else. Thinking about a television commercial that he saw advertised but the product escaped him, he thought about the jingle and how appropriate it was for the moment—*whatever you do, don't let them see you sweat.*

Amanda rescued him from his lack of ability to speak. Lenny and Amanda looked at each other a minute too long. Lenny merely nodded his head. Lenny thought, how stupid was that. He had to get a grip on his emotions.

"Hello Lenny. Nice to meet you."

Strangely, Woody looked at Lenny and then at Amanda. Woody did not know if it was his imagination or his paranoia but something told him that Amanda and Lenny already knew each other. Woody decided to put the question out there, not really asking either one of them directly.

"Do you two know each other?"

"I..." Amanda knew she had waited too long to answer. It was Lenny who rescued Amanda this time and answered for both of them.

Lenny added, "We sort of know each other. I drive the city bus and Amanda was one of my bus passengers. I should have said, she used to ride my bus."

"That's right." Letting out a nervous laugh, Amanda pressed on.

"When I saw Lenny enter through the sliding glass doors, I was trying to figure out why he looked so familiar. Woody, remember when I used to take the bus to work?" It was a rhetorical question.

"Well, I used to take Lenny's bus. Because he was so friendly with all his bus riders, I learned that his name was Lenny Harper. That's how we know each other."

Amanda was talking too fast and basically repeated what Lenny had said about how they knew each other. She could barely look at Lenny. And it was out of the question to look directly at Woody. It would have been too easy for Woody to detect that she was not totally telling the truth and right now she was bordering between the truth and a lie.

Listening to Amanda ramble on about how she knew Lenny, Woody thought about that old saying, *"I might be old but I'm not stupid. His mama didn't raise no fool."* That may be how his wife met Lenny Harper but the tension going on between the two of them told him something totally different. Starting to say something, Woody changed his mind. He decided to watch the exchange of words between his wife and Lenny.

In addition, something told Woody that this was neither the time nor the place for any more questions regarding the relationship of the two of them. Besides he was not one to make false accusations. If there were more going on between Amanda and Lenny, he would find out what they were hiding. Then he would ask his wife about Lenny.

There was an uncomfortable silence as Amanda took a quick glance at Lenny. Amanda was glad Lenny had moved on with his life but she could not help but feel a tinge of jealousy as she looked at the attractive woman he had brought with him. Standing between Woody and Lenny, she felt awkward. Amanda didn't have a clue as to how to continue talking but some how she managed to say.

"So, how are you doing?"

"I'm fine. Still, driving the bus."

Without hesitation Lenny responded but with a short, crisp answer. As time passed, Lenny regained his full composure. Lenny had forgotten about Eloise.

"Forgive my manners, did I introduce you to Eloise?" Lenny grabbed her hand. He was glad to be able to focus on someone else.

Quickly Lenny added, "and by the way, she's Austin's younger sister."

Turning his attention to Eloise, Woody fixed his eyes admiringly on a pretty brown skinned woman with long flowing hair.

"Another surprise. Well thank goodness you don't look like your brother."

Although everyone laughed, it was the doorbell that seemed to save the moment. Woody turned and excused himself as he went to answer the door. When Woody turned to leave, Amanda excused herself and turned her attention to the blender that was on the bar counter.

Taking the opportunity to sit down, Lenny led Eloise across the lanai to two chairs in the corner. Their seats were across from Justin and his wife.

As Eloise and Lenny sat down, his tone was insistent. "I need to tell you something."

"What's wrong?" Eloise could see he was upset but she had no idea why.

Glancing around and making sure no one could hear him, he spoke and lowered his voice to a whisper. "Amanda is Mandy."

"What?" Eloise let out an unanticipated loud response. Several people focused their eyes on her outburst. Not paying attention to anyone else, Eloise apologized to Lenny.

She spoke softly. "Did you know that Amanda…"

"Do I really look that stupid?" Annoyed Lenny reacted through gritted teeth.

"I had no idea she was married to Woody. When I saw Mandy…Amanda, I was just as stunned as she was."

He did not wait for a reply. "Not to mention, I never knew her by Amanda. She always called herself Mandy and she never told me her last name."

Lenny looked over his shoulder to make sure no one could hear their conversation.

Lenny asked, "by any chance did you pay attention to Woody as far as his reaction to what Amanda told him about how she knew me?"

"No. Not really." Eloise was not completely truthful with Lenny. There was no need in making him feel any worse than he did.

When Eloise looked at Amanda she could see how Lenny was unable to have resisted her charms. She was an attractive woman with an unusual style to her. She had to have been no taller than five feet tall but yet she appeared taller. For someone with her dark skin tone, she was able to wear a short blond hair cut. Eloise put Amanda in the category of being a *"Diva."* There was no question that she commanded a room with such flair that she was able to gain the attention from men, as well as women.

For some reason Lenny did not believe Eloise. He asked again.

"Are you sure Woody believed us?"

"Well, you might have given him reason to pause and question how you knew each other."

"What did I do?"

"Well, there were several times when you were stumbling all over your words and it seemed as though you couldn't talk, let alone answer questions. So if anything, you might have given him reason to suspect that something wasn't quite kosher about how the two of you know each other."

"Oh great." Lenny exhaled.

Without talking directly to Eloise he said, "What a mess."

Justin and Suzanne were watching Lenny and Eloise closely. Leaning into Suzanne, Justin spoke in a low tone.

"It seems like Amanda knows everybody. First she knew me, and now Lenny. This has certainly turned into an interesting afternoon."

"You're telling me. It goes to show you that this is a small, small world."

CHAPTER 43

"Everybody, may I have your attention?" Heads turned toward Woody as he spoke.

"I would like to introduce Bob and Vanessa Webster." Woody took them to the bar, and formally introduced them to Amanda who was busy fixing more Margarita drinks.

"Welcome to our home."

"Amanda I'm so happy that you took the initiative to have the husbands and their significant others over so we could meet one another. Your home is so warm and welcoming."

"Thank you. It was nothing having everyone over."

"Oh yes it was and I really appreciate it. Now I can put the men's names with their faces. Moreover I wanted to see what was all the hoopla about the men golfing on Sundays."

"I know what you mean. This is the first time in a long time since I've seen Woody so excited about doing anything, especially with men."

"Well, Bob knows plenty of men, but this is the first time that men have been able to keep my man from spending time with me on Sunday mornings." Bob rolled his eyes. He could not believe she said that.

"Amanda, can I have a beer, something light please?" She handed him the beer.

"Thanks."

As Bob got his beer, he strolled over to where Justin and his wife were sitting. Vanessa shrugged it off but she wished Bob had stayed by her side while she continued her conversation with Amanda. Not wanting to appear possessive, Vanessa stayed where she was and kept talking to Amanda.

"Hi Justin."

"Hey Bob. This is my wife Suzanne."

"Pleased to meet you. How long have you been here?"

"About fifteen minutes. We arrived shortly after Russell and his wife. It's really a nice afternoon and Woody and his wife have really put out the red carpet."

"The Villages is something isn't it? When I retire, I could do this."

"I know what you mean but I've got a long time before I can even think about retirement."

"Me too. I just got married."

"We haven't been married that long either. Not to mention we're expecting a baby."

Suzanne smiled. She was taken back when Justin told Bob about her pregnancy. This was the first sign she had gotten from Justin that he had accepted the fact that they were going to have a baby. That made her happy. Raising her eyes upward, she took a minute and quickly said, *"Thank you God for small blessings."*

"Congratulations man."

The room was full of chatter and laughter as the doorbell rang again. No one seemed to hear it except for Woody as he exited the lanai to answer it.

CHAPTER 44

When Woody answered the door and saw Donnie, he had to admit that Donnie's partner did not look anything like he expected. The man who Donnie introduced to him as Raymond did not look gay. Raymond had to be at least six feet four inches tall, incredibly athletically built, and had looks that would turn any woman's head.

Woody was sure that when women found out that he was not interested in their gender, they probably thought what a waste. If Woody had met this man without knowing he was gay he would never have guessed it. There was nothing about him that suggested, "gay." His looks and tenor voice certainly did not reek of anything but masculinity. Despite what Woody thought, he flipped his wrist and exaggerated the introduction. It did not go unnoticed.

"Everyone, Donnie and Ray—Mon are here."

Not wanting Woody to continue Donnie took over the introductions. Raymond did not hide the fact that he was not pleased to be at the brunch and did not appreciate Woody's humor. After the introductions Raymond leaned into Donnie and whispered.

"If you want me to survive through this afternoon and if you don't want me to kill Woody, you better get me something alcoholic to drink quick."

"Don't let Woody get under your skin. I think he likes you."

Letting out a small snicker, Donnie grabbed Raymond's hand and walked to the bar. Approaching the bar, Raymond stopped dead in his tracks for a minute. He squinted at Vanessa.

"Oh my! How long has it been? I can't believe my eyes?"

All conversations stopped. All eyes were on Raymond as he dramatically talked to Bob Webster's wife.

Woody changed his mind about Raymond not sounding "gay." As Raymond continued talking to Bob's wife, his voice got an octave higher with each word that came out of his mouth. Raymond had put his hand on his hip and Woody watched with anticipation. His stance took on feminine moves. At any moment, Woody was sure Raymond was going to do the finger-snapping, head rolling routine he had seen done so often by black comedians who imitated the so called "ghetto black woman" when she exaggerated certain moves when making a point.

"Vanessa Louise Tanner, my, my, my."

"I'm sorry I don't recognize..."

"Pleassse. Raymond Walker from Trinity High School, the class of..."

Loudly laughing, Vanessa was able to stop Raymond before he had a chance to say the year they graduated. Apprehensively, Vanessa strolled over to Raymond. By the time she had reached him she had regrouped. Vanessa gave Raymond an insincere hug and then cheek kisses. Letting go of the embrace, Vanessa looked at Raymond.

"How could I have forgotten you? It's just that when you haven't seen a person in a long time. It's hard to remember names once you're out of high school." Letting out a tense laugh, Vanessa thought she needed to stop talking aimlessly.

"Crazy me. Now that I look at you, you haven't changed one bit since you graduated from high school. In addition, you still look as good as ever." Not knowing what else to say Vanessa grabbed Raymond by the arm and ushered him over to Bob.

You did not have to hit Raymond over the head with a big stick to understand that Vanessa did not want anyone to know her age. Looking at Vanessa's husband, Raymond figured she must have been at least five years older than him. He wondered why she was concerned about their age difference because she certainly had kept herself looking good. In fact to Raymond, she looked better now than she did in high school.

Raymond thought to himself, she needed to get with it. Just recently Oprah had women from all walks of life on her show talking about dating and marrying younger men. Many of the couples had been married for 15 years or longer. But for some reason Vanessa was not cool with it. Raymond smiled. He knew how to keep a secret.

Vanessa hoped Raymond would stop all the chatter about when they went to high school. Once the year they graduated was out, there would be no guessing. It would be easy to do the numbers. She thought to herself how you could hide but you cannot run. Sooner or later, the truth had a way of catching up with you.

Through all the chaos, someone said loudly, "Someone's at the door. The doorbell is ringing."

CHAPTER 45

Billy Ray, Austin and two women entered. Since Woody had not answered the door, he had no idea who was a couple. Amanda had stopped in the kitchen to check on the peach cobbler. Hearing Woody making the introductions, Amanda was too late to stop him.

"May I have everyone's attention for a moment?" Billy Ray and Austin have arrived. Since Billy Ray was standing next to Woody, he did not see Billy Ray holding Ebony's hand. So Woody turned to the white woman who was standing beside him and made the introduction.

"Everyone this is Billy Ray and his wife."

Woody, like so many other people, had assumed that the white woman was Billy Ray's wife. Quickly Amanda stepped in.

"Actually, Ebony is Billy Ray's wife. And Jessica is Austin's wife."

"Sorry, my bag." Woody looked at Austin and then at Billy Ray.

"How was I supposed to know? It was an honest mistake," Woody said under his breath. He turned and walked away.

Before anything else was said, Austin and Ebony spotted their sister Eloise almost at the same time. In unison they spoke to her.

"Hey Eloise."

Austin hugged and kissed his sister on the cheek. When he let go of the embrace, Ebony gave her a hug.

"I'm surprised to see you here." Austin winked at her. In a playful manner, she frowned at her brother.

"I might be your baby sister but I'm three times seven and plus some. Therefore, I don't have to tell you everything."

Looking at Billy Ray, Eloise could see that he was still fuming over the mistake made by Woody. Billy Ray had his attention on Woody as if he was about to pounce on him. Deciding to defuse what could turn into an unnecessary round of hurtful words, Eloise chastised her brother and brother-in-law with a little humor.

"From the puzzled looks and astonished faces around the room, you two didn't tell anyone that you were brothers-in-law." With a raised eyebrow, Eloise looked at Austin and Billy Ray as she wagged her finger at them.

"Shame on you two."

Nervously everyone laughed. Where the room had been a party atmosphere, now there were whispers and stares. Eloise was sure that no one cared that Billy Ray and Austin were in interracial marriages. The shock was that they had hidden the fact that they were brothers-in-law.

Now Woody understood why Austin, a black man and Billy Ray, a white man, were so cool with each other. Billy Ray was married to Austin's sister. Woody thought that Austin sure did keep a lot of secrets. Woody wondered when Lenny started dating Austin's sister. That was a surprise and no one knew until Lenny arrived at the brunch and introduced her to everyone.

When Woody thought about it, if Austin wanted to keep his family a mystery it was his business. Woody thought the biggest secret was how attractive his sisters were. With sisters that fine, Woody could not begin to understand how Austin ended up with a white woman as his wife? His wife was the typical looking white woman—blonde hair, little to thin for his taste, light blue eyes, and sort of plain looking. To him, she did not fall in the pretty category.

Looking at Lenny, Austin thought he appeared as though he was deep in thought. Something was definitely bothering him.

"Lenny, you seem a little preoccupied. Is everything okay?"

Physically Lenny was fine but emotionally he was a wreck. All he could think about was when could he leave. He wanted the afternoon to end as soon as possible.

Softly he replied, "I'm okay. Just tired, I guess." Lenny gave Austin a weak smile.

As Amanda glanced around the room, she was worried. Without a doubt the happy chatter and laughter had vacated the room. When she thought the afternoon could not get any worse, her husband had to make the God-awful mistake of introducing the wrong wives with the wrong husbands.

The room seemed to be filled with people somewhat on the edge. Amanda was trying to avoid any more mishaps. At any moment it seemed as though someone may be on the brink of going off on someone. As hostess it was her job to get everyone back into a festive party mood.

"Since everyone's here now, let's eat. The food is set up in the dining room. There's plenty of food. Please eat up or Woody and I will be eating the leftovers for the next week."

Everyone appeared to be relieved to be able to do something other than talk. Single file, they entered into the dining room and saw a beautifully set buffet style table. The table had fresh flowers, crystal glasses and plates, and candles strategically lit around the room. Amanda had told the truth about the abundance of food. She must have thought she was feeding an army.

There was an array of chicken—grilled, fried, and barbeque, grilled shrimp, sliced turkey and ham, roast beef, fruit and green salads, potato and macaroni salad, bake beans, grilled vegetables, and rolls. Then there was a table filled with an assortment of desserts—pies, cakes, cookies, brownies, banana pudding, and peach cobbler. The table was a feast fit for a king. Everyone complimented Amanda on the table and the food.

While everyone was eating, Woody had put on some upbeat

SUNDAY GOLF

rhythm and blues music. When everyone finished eating, some couples began to dance. Amanda began to relax. When the electric slide came on, she got everyone, to do the popular line dance, except for Russell and his wife. Before everyone could sit down, Amanda persuaded everyone to form a Soul Train Line. The men tried to out do one another in demonstrating their dance moves. When it was Woody's turn, he did a rendition of James Brown's steps. He even did a split.

At that point, everyone started shouting, "Go Woody. Go Woody."

From the looks on the men's faces, Amanda knew they were surprised that Woody could dance and was so light on his feet. Amanda smiled and thought. *"For his age, he still had the moves."* The music had saved the day. Amanda was relieved that the afternoon had not been a total disaster.

She had planned and had expected a pleasant afternoon where everyone would get to meet one another. Instead, it had turned out to be an afternoon full of surprises and apparently secrets that some people did not want revealed, including her. If she had not taken the Prozac earlier, she would have lost her cool the moment she saw Lenny.

When the last person left Amanda was in high spirits and exhausted to the point that every bone in her body was longing for a rest. To say the afternoon had been stressful was an understatement.

CHAPTER 46

Woody gave Amanda a tight hug. He kissed her deeply. He was appreciative of her efforts for having the brunch. Everyone seemed to have had a good time. Releasing his grip, he wanted her to know what he thought of the brunch.

"Thanks dear for having all those people over."

"It was nothing Woody. You know I love to entertain."

"Did you notice how tense some of the men and their wives were?"

"Yes I did." Amanda did not want Woody to get on the subject of her and Lenny.

Quickly, she steered the conversation to someone else. "I didn't have a chance to tell you about Justin Williams."

"What about him?"

"I prosecuted him."

"You're joking?"

"No. He was sentenced to five years in prison. When I saw him, I was blown away. At first, all I could think about was how he might want to hurt me—you know revenge. Then I regrouped realizing that Justin had no idea that I was your wife. But for a minute, I was more than nervous. I was scared."

"I'm sorry. You should have said something."

"I guess I should have but I didn't want to upset anyone, especially his wife. I take it none of the men knew about him spending time in prison."

"No. We—let me speak for me. I had no idea. Well, did you put him away for a violent crime?"

"Well, no but his friends made the crime violent when they shot a man but he didn't die." Amanda's eyes clouded over as she tried to recall the case.

"If I remember correctly Justin was supposed to be the look out for his friends while they robbed the bank. However, once they went inside the bank, Justin got cold feet and drove away in the get-away car. He left the scene of the crime. That's why he didn't get a harsh sentencing."

"Hmmm. That doesn't sound right to me. I know the case is over but why did Justin have to serve any time? He did leave. He wasn't there when the crime was committed?"

"Forgive me Woody but I don't remember all the details of the case but it had something to do with Justin's friends stating that he was the mastermind behind the robbery. I'm sorry, with all the cases I handle I just don't remember all of the details." Amanda shrugged her shoulders.

Woody commented, "Well, he looks like he's turned his life around. His wife certainly seems personable."

"She does seem nice. What did you think about Russell's wife?"

Woody thought for a minute and then said, "One word—controlling. Not to mention, she was reserved, cold, and aggressive. She and Russell sat in that one spot all afternoon. When you said that the food was being served I wasn't even sure they were going to eat anything. The only time they socialized was when someone sat down next to them."

Amanda started laughing.

"What's so funny?"

"You. Woody, when you mistakenly introduced Austin's wife as

Billy Ray's wife. I thought I would die."

"That wasn't funny."

"Yes it was because the look on your face was indescribable. You looked like you didn't know whether to laugh or cry when I stepped in and told you which woman was with which man."

"Well, I'm sure that wasn't the first time that someone thought that Austin was with his sister and vice versus. I know that it won't be the last time that when the four of them are out together that someone makes that assumption. It was an honest mistake."

"I know but you should have seen your face, along with the other men's faces."

"Oh I think the men were reacting to the fact that Billy Ray and Austin are brothers-in-law. For some reason those two kept that a secret. And Austin's sister dates Lenny." When Woody mentioned Lenny's name, he watched Amanda closely. There was no reaction.

"It's certainly a small world. Like me knowing Lenny." Amanda prayed Woody would not ask her any more questions about Lenny. She waited giving him time to say something else about Lenny. When he did not, she was thankful when he started talking about someone else.

"What did you think about Ray—Mon?" Woody bent his wrist and sauntered across the room. Amanda laughed.

"You should stop that."

Amanda continued, "besides, I could not believe you called that man Ray—Mon instead of Raymond. You have to admit, Donnie and Raymond make an attractive couple. They were very sociable. I had a blast talking to Donnie."

"You didn't answer my question. What did you think about Raymond?"

"I have to confess I thought at first he was very masculine. But then when he recognized Vanessa, he forgot all about being a man and went into a routine that caused him to act and talk more like a woman than a man."

"I could barely refrain myself from laughing."

"You and everyone else."

After Amanda put the last food in the refrigerator, she started picking up the dirty glasses and dishes, empty soda and beer cans. As she was about to load the dishwasher Woody stopped her.

"Amanda, let's go to bed. Since I'm home all day there's no reason why I can't clean up tomorrow. It's been a long day."

He grabbed her hand and led her to the master bedroom. They embraced and kissed. Amanda looked up into Woody's eyes.

"Woody, I hope you know I love you very much. I would never deliberately do anything to hurt you."

Woody said nothing. He released his wife. They undressed in silence. Woody got in the bed and continued to watch his beautiful wife get undressed. After taking off her make-up and brushing her teeth, she got into bed. They kissed and he held her tightly.

Whispering he said in Amanda's ear. "I love you too. I know you haven't done anything that would hurt me or our marriage."

Amanda froze. She bit her lip hard, hoping she could hold back the tears. She wanted to tell Woody about her infidelity but then she thought what would be accomplished? Why talk about something that's over? She had ended the affair. Most of all, there was never a moment when she had planned on leaving him. She saw no reason to confess her sins in an effort to clear her conscience. At that moment, she swore to a higher power that she would never reveal her infidelity to anyone.

CHAPTER 47

"Give me the car keys" Connie growled. As they walked to the parked car, she insisted on driving. However, Russell wanted to drive because he could visibly see she was angry, from the way her lips were pursed tightly and her jaws were clenched.

As usual, Russell was clueless as to why or what might have made her angry. It was not like they did a lot of socializing at the brunch. He saw no reason for her to have an attitude. Driving out of The Villages, Connie seemed to be concentrating on the directions to County Road 446. As a result, she was not engaging him in conversation until she eased to a complete stop at the red light. Then without warning, and as hard as she could, she gave Russell a backhanded slap that landed directly on his face. Russell felt the impact and flinched. He said nothing. As the light turned green, Connie started yelling.

"What did you tell those men about me?"

Barely above a whisper, Russell answered, "nothing."

Not paying attention to the upcoming traffic light, Connie slammed on the brakes. The light turned red as she stopped. The abrupt stop made both Connie and Russell lunge forward. As Russell sat back, Connie balled up her hand and hit Russell again using her fist. This time, the blow was with more force.

"I'm asking you again, what did you tell those men? I saw how they looked at me."

The light turned green and Connie drove slowly through the light. Glancing at Russell, she saw him touching the side of his face. Connie's last blow had broken the skin on Russell's mouth. He felt a small amount of blood oozing from his lip. Taking out a handkerchief, he dabbed at the blood. The next two traffic lights, Connie made no effort to hit Russell. Connie's hand was hurting. She guessed the pain was either from her gripping the steering wheel too tightly or from hitting Russell.

Connie had been out of control for years but yet she had no recollection as to why she was angry. She did know that ever since she married Russell, he seemed to be the target of her rage. The harder she tried not to strike him the more difficult it was for her to control her emotions. She loved him but it was not enough for her to stop hitting him when she lost her temper. Connie had lowered her tone, but her voice was still roaring.

"Tell me about that man's wife who is the counselor for abused women."

Defiantly Russell looked at Connie.

"I don't know any more about Justin's wife than you do. I never met her until today." Russell swore he felt heat escaping from her mouth when she screamed.

"You're a liar. I found her business card in your pant pocket."

Russell did not know how to respond. He thought he had hidden the business card. It did not matter because she knew about it now.

Calmly, he tried to explain. "Listen. It's not what you think."

Russell noticed Connie was speeding and said, "Connie slow down."

"Don't you tell me how to drive," she yelled.

Then she attempted to grab Russell, his reflex caused him to pull away. At that moment Connie took her eyes off the road. She put her foot on the brake but she had to swerve the car to miss running head on into a tree. Thinking they were out of trouble, Connie did not see the large tree stump that caused the car to flip. As the car turned over, it landed in a ditch beside the road.

Russell was barely conscious and the air bag was pressed against his chest so he could hardly move. His entire upper body was immobile. Carefully he tried to turn his head, but a pain shot up his spine. If he had injuries, he did not want to worsen them. Instead of moving again, he moved his eyes from side to side but he couldn't see anything, especially the driver's seat. He was trying to locate Connie. He called out to her but his voice was more like a mumble.

"Connie can you hear me?"

There was no answer. Russell tried several more times but without success. Connie was not responding.

He decided to conserve his energy rather than to continue calling out to his wife who apparently was incapable of answering his calls. He did the only thing he could do and that was to pray. No sooner had Russell said a prayer—asking God for help when he thought he heard a voice.

"Can anyone hear me?"

It was a voice—a man's voice was yelling louder so that Russell was able to hear him. Without moving his head, Russell could see the man peeping through the car window. Russell was thankful that someone had come to rescue them.

Overcome by emotions Russell felt tears rolling down his cheeks. When Russell tried to answer the man, he found no sound coming forth. Again the male voice called out.

"Can anyone hear me?"

From somewhere Russell found inner strength that helped him to speak. The sound was raspy and low. "I can hear you. I'm pinned down."

Stopping, Russell grasped for some air.

"My wife is in the car with me but I can't see her. She's not responding. Please help her."

"Well, just take it easy. The Paramedics should be here shortly. I called 911 when I saw your car flip. They will get you out as soon as possible. Hang in there."

Between the time Russell talked to the man and the Paramedics arriving at the scene of the accident, he lost consciousness. Russell did not remember being pulled out of the car. The next memory Russell had was being in Leesburg Regional Medical Center. As he looked around, he was in a hospital room, not in the emergency room. He wondered how long he had been unconscious.

"Mr. Allen, can you hear me?" A man in a white coat was talking to him. Russell assumed it was a doctor.

"Yes. How's my wife?"

"She's going to be fine." From Mr. Allen's facial expression, the doctor thought he better give him a more detailed explanation.

"Your wife suffered a number of broken bones and bruises. She just got out of surgery. The worse of her injuries was the broken hip, arm, and leg but she's going to be okay."

"When can I go home?"

"Oh you need to stay here at least for 24 hours observation. That means you'll be here at least over night. Although you only had some superficial bruises, you did suffer a nasty hit on the head. That's probably why your head hurts. I'm sure you'll be able to go home tomorrow."

"I need to talk to my children. I know they're worried."

"They're okay. I talked to your brother and sister-in-law about you and your wife's condition. In addition, it's my understanding that they have your children. All I want you to do Mr. Allen is get some rest."

The next day Russell was released from the hospital. He did not bother visiting Connie. Instead he went directly to his brother's house to pick up Joey and Joy. He wanted his children to see him so they could see for themselves that he was okay.

"Were you worried about mommy and daddy?"

Joey said, "Yes daddy but Uncle Fred said you were okay."

Russell twirled around to show the twins that he was doing fine. He hugged Joey and Joy and tickled them. They laughed.

"As you can see daddy's fine except for some cuts and bruises.

Mommy is going to be okay too."

"Where is mommy?"

"She's in the hospital. She has to stay in there for a little while. Maybe I can arrange for you to visit her. Okay?"

Joey and Joy seemed like they understood and they were relieved to see him. Russell thanked his brother and sister-in-law and took his children home. It was days before Russell visited Connie. Constantly, she phoned the house and ordered him to come to the hospital but he ignored her demands. After what had happened, he wanted to spend time with the children.

Finally, when Russell did visit Connie, she was wearing a frown and immediately she went into an instant assault mode.

"I've been calling you. Where have you been?"

Russell ignored the question. He thought she should be grateful to be alive after what she put them through. Unnecessarily, she had caused an accident that could have killed them because of her anger. Instead of gratitude, out of her mouth spilled nothing but nastiness. It took everything Russell had to be civil.

"How are you feeling?"

"How do you think I'm feeling?" Connie answered with a snide remark.

"Well, I'm sorry you suffered so many injuries. I understand you'll be in the hospital for several weeks and then you have to have rehabilitation."

"I guess you're happy about that?"

"Look I'm not going to argue with you Connie. I'll see you tomorrow. I need to get home and take care of Joey and Joy."

"Joey and Joy—I'm the one with needs. You should be concerned about me."

Russell felt sorry for Connie. She was such an unhappy person. He looked at her and merely shook his head. He turned his back to her as he walked toward the door.

"Don't you dare turn your back on me while I'm still talking to

you, Russell LeRoy Allen. There are…"
 Walking out the room, Russell kept going. He left Connie talking to his back.

CHAPTER 48

The accident was a wake up call for Russell. There was nothing else he could do but to take charge of his life. As much as he was against divorce especially when children were involved, he decided that in this case he had no alternative. If he continued to expose his children to arguing and beatings, what chance would they have in developing into normal, healthy adults?

Russell had contemplated long enough about he and Connie. Their marriage was dysfunctional. Before his love for her turned into hate, he had to divorce her. If anything, Russell only saw more disaster. Connie needed help. If he continued to stay with her, he now recognized how much she was endangering his and the children's lives.

Calling Suzanne, Russell knew that was his first step. He wanted to make a change. He could not continue to let his life be in constant turmoil. If nothing else, he had to start a new beginning for his children.

"Hello."

"Hello Justin." Russell recognized his deep voice.

"Justin, it's Russell."

Excitedly, Justin said, "Hey man. How are you doing?"

"I'm doing better."

Justin had already heard about the accident but no one seemed to know any of the details and the hospital only gave out general information. Justin was glad to hear from him.

"I'm sorry to hear about you and Connie. How is she doing?"

Russell let out a chuckle. "Madder than hell. Secretly, I think she wished it had been me who suffered all the broken bones. Was I interrupting anything?"

"Not really. Why?"

"I was wondering if I could speak to Suzanne?"

"Sure. Let me get her. Listen, if you need anything, let me know."

"Thanks man." Within a few minutes Suzanne picked up the phone.

"Hi Suzanne."

"Hi Russell. How are you doing? And Connie how is she?"

"I don't know if Justin had time to tell you but the short version is that Connie is doing fine despite some broken bones. I'm physically fine and each day I feel better. We were lucky we escaped with just bruises and broken bones. She could have killed us."

"Maybe that's what she was trying to do."

"Please, don't say that." Russell could not fathom the thought that Connie would be so insensitive.

"Russell, I'm sorry but she does appear to be more out of control and more violent, each time she does something to you."

"I know but I hate to think that her actions would result in our children being without parents."

"What can I do to help Russell?"

"I'll get right to the point. I need a good lawyer. I thought about what you told me about leaving and moving to another city but I'm not going to run. Why should I uproot my children and change my entire life? No, I have decided, I won't do it. If anyone makes any changes, it will be Connie."

"Okay but . . . " Suzanne did not want to discourage Russell but dealing with Connie will not be an easy feat.

"I have a plan. After our initial meeting and you explained to me what my options were, I started giving my situation a lot of thought."

"Good for you. It's not that I don't have a good lawyer but given the circumstances I'm not sure you…"

"Trust me Suzanne. All I need is a lawyer who can draw up some legal documents, separation and divorce papers."

"There is a lawyer who works for our church. Generally, he helps the abused women who are ready to take some legal action regarding their situations. He can definitely help you. I just want you to be sure."

"Oh I'm sure. She nearly killed us and she never once thought about our children. She's a malicious, hateful, bully who needs help." Russell's words were full of malice.

"When can I meet with the lawyer?"

"I'm not sure but why the hurry?"

"I want to do this before I change my mind." Suzanne smiled.

She had an idea and said, "Russell, if I can get you an appointment with the lawyer maybe you can serve Connie the papers while she's in the hospital."

Nervously, Russell responded, "Oh, I hadn't thought about serving her the papers."

"It will be okay and this is the best way to deal with her. Now, I'm not sure when I can get you an appointment or if the lawyer can work that fast. Usually, these situations take time but since you're not going to be moving out of town, maybe…" Russell did not let Suzanne finish her sentence.

"Suzanne what you don't realize is that I have evidence against Connie. As a result, I think she will agree to the divorce and she will give me full custody of the children."

Hearing what Russell said, Suzanne became concerned. She hoped he was not setting himself up for disappointment. Carefully Suzanne chose her words.

"Russell, you sound very confident and that's good but…" Russell stopped her.

"Listen after watching the OJ Simpson trial, I went to great lengths taking pictures and recording the date and any significant details regarding each time Connie beat me."

"But she could dispute the pictures." Suzanne did not want to sound pessimistic but she had seen too many cases turn against the accuser. He needed to understand what he would be up against.

"You don't know Connie. You see she was the first black woman promoted into a managerial job. She loves power. Currently, she is about to get promoted and she will do anything to keep that position. This is probably the best opportunity I will ever have to obtain a quiet divorce and full custody of my children."

Suzanne listened as Russell explained. "I'll send the pictures to her boss. Her job has a very strict moral clause. They'll ask her to resign."

Suzanne had to admit Russell had a well-thought out plan. She admired him. Although Suzanne did not know all the legal ramifications, it sounded as though Russell had a strong case. Suzanne also agreed with Russell in that he had to move quickly. Suzanne hated to say it but Russell had to take action while Connie was vulnerable. This way he would be in complete control.

From experience of working with abused women, Suzanne knew that he needed to act while he had the courage to carry out his plan. Too often Suzanne had seen women with viable plans but let their spouses convince them that things would change. In the end, many of the women returned to their spouses and unfortunately, the cycle of physical abuse started all over again.

CHAPTER 49

It took several days before Suzanne could arrange a meeting between Russell and the lawyer. Once he met with the lawyer everything was put into motion—a restraining order was filed, Connie's belongings were moved out of the house and put into storage, and separation papers were drawn up.

It had been over two weeks and Connie was still in the hospital. Unfortunately, Connie had suffered an infection, an allergic reaction to the antibiotic to treat the infection, and she had not been able to receive any physical therapy.

While Connie was still in the hospital, Suzanne suggested that Russell present the restraining order and legal separation papers to her. Outside the hospital room, Russell hesitated. Suzanne prayed he had not lost his courage.

"Russell, are you okay?" He merely nodded his head.

"If you want, we can wait until another day. The separation papers are good for thirty days."

"No. I'm okay. Just give me a minute."

Suzanne urged, "Inhale, exhale. Quit holding your breath. Remember, there is nothing she can do to you Russell."

"I know but…" Russell stopped. He had to do this if not for him then for his children.

"Let's go." He opened the door.

When they entered the room, Connie was sitting up in bed. Looking at her, Russell thought she looked so vulnerable. For a second, thoughts were going through his head of not giving her the papers until she was released from the hospital. After what seemed like a long silence Russell finally spoke. His legs were shaking. He hoped Connie could not see his nervousness.

"Good morning Connie."

"What's good about it and what is she doing here?" she asked.

"I asked her to be here."

Russell looked at Suzanne. She smiled and nodded at him to give him support. He cleared his throat.

Connie asked, "For what? What's going on?" She glared at Russell and then at Suzanne.

"Connie, calm down and I'll explain. Connie, we have not been getting along for some time." Russell let out a heavy sigh. He had to hurry up and get through this before he lost his nerve. When he looked at the scowl on Connie's face, he felt his knees buckle.

"Says who?"

"Come on Connie. You know we have some problems and I can't do this any more."

"What problems, if you mean the small altercations that we have had from time to time, well that's not that unusual."

Connie stopped and looked at Russell. To Russell, he saw nothing but Connie's feeble attempt to dismiss his concerns.

"How about a marriage counselor?" She threw the question out as if to pacify Russell.

"For what?" When he answered her with a question, Russell saw the all too familiar face of Connie that was twisted into an expression of hatred. At that moment, something snapped and Russell started talking with confidence. He did not give her an opportunity to speak.

However, when he finished, Connie spouted out so many obscenities and threats that Suzanne was speechless. She could not recall ever experiencing seeing or hearing so much hostility in one person.

There was one last piece of business Russell had to do and that was to give Connie the restraining and separation papers. When Russell handed the documents to Connie, she grabbed them from him.

She roared, "What are these?"

"The documents are self-explanatory." Russell responded in a crisp, poised manner.

Suddenly, Connie's mannerism had changed. The lines on her face had softened and her voice was now sweet and tender.

"This is so overwhelming to me. Russell, I had no idea you felt this way." A tear fell down her cheek as she looked at Russell. Russell wanted to believe her. She looked so helpless.

"If this is what you want I understand but I would like to discuss this when it's just the two of us." Russell was noncommittal as he looked at her and then at Suzanne who shook her head.

"Well, I should be going." As he and Suzanne turned to leave, they heard Connie. It sounded as if she was crying.

"Before you go, Russell would you be so kind as to raise my pillow behind my head. I'd really appreciate it."

Apprehensively Russell approached the bed. Raising the pillow, he did not see Connie's balled up fist. Swinging at him, Connie attempted to hit him with all her force. Instinctively, Russell jerked back. With Russell pulling back and the weight of her various casts, Connie lost her balance and fell backwards. Everything happened so fast that Russell and Suzanne were unable to prevent her from tumbling out the bed.

She yelled, "Look what you've done? You're a moron."

"Get the nurse. I think I've broken something. You'll pay for this Russell. You just wait." She was screaming at the top of her lungs.

As Russell and Suzanne were about to help Connie, two nurses rushed through the door. Immediately, the nurses assisted Connie. When they were getting her back in the bed, she was shouting.

"Be careful. That hurts. Get a doctor. I need help now."

Before the nurses could respond to Connie's request, a nurse and a doctor appeared in the room to see what all the commotion was about. The doctor conducted a quick exam and instructed one of the nurses to take Connie to the x-ray room. It appeared as though the fall may have caused her to sustain new injuries.

Before Connie could notice, Russell and Suzanne had slipped out the room, leaving her screaming at anyone who was near her. As they walked down the hospital corridor, Suzanne asked out of curiosity.

"How do you feel Russell?"

He didn't know how to answer Suzanne. He had mixed emotions. He was happy that he could get on with his life but he was sad. While they waited for the elevator, he responded.

"I feel sorry for Connie, mainly because of the twins and the fact that she needs help and she can't admit it. However, he could not suppress his happiness as he smiled at Suzanne.

"What?"

"For the first time since my children were born, we can begin to live without fear."

When Russell got home he had a message from Lenny. The guys were going to meet at Perkins to discuss golfing on Sundays. Unfortunately, he would no longer be able to join them. With the separation, he needed to spend as much time as possible with his children.

CHAPTER 50

As soon as Amanda left for work, Woody would start his mission. For the past several weeks, he had been tearing the house apart. He was trying to find anything that might link Amanda to Lenny Harper. Woody had a gut feeling that Amanda and Lenny had an affair. So far he had been unable to prove it. He had not asked Amanda primarily because he was not prepared to hear the answer.

Today, Woody decided he would look on Amanda's computer. They each had a computer and up until now Woody never would have thought about snooping around in Amanda's home office. But Woody was curious about whether she had a relationship with Lenny. Woody hired a detective but he had uncovered nothing. Rather than pay more money for the detective to find nothing, Woody decided he would conduct his own investigation.

When Woody switched Amanda's computer on, the opening screen demanded a password. He should have known her computer would be password protected. Trying several passwords—Manda, Mandy, Manda Bear—nothing. Woody was not having much success.

He looked in the desk drawers and in the file cabinet. While looking under the desk blotter, Woody accidentally knocked over the telephone. As luck would have it, there stuck on the bottom of the telephone was her password. Of all the passwords, she had chosen—menopause.

Now that he was in her computer, what was he looking for? It was not like he was that computer literate. He looked at her email—nothing. He looked at a number of programs but found nothing. Getting discouraged, he was about to turn off the computer when he saw something titled, *"My documents."* He clicked on *"My documents"* and there he found the incriminating evidence—a letter to Mr. Harper. Well, he got what he wanted.

As Woody read the letter, he was crushed. Never in a million years would he have imagined that Amanda would have had an affair. He could not believe she had jeopardized their marriage and everything they had for a romp in the bed.

Yes, Woody knew he was almost 20 years older than Amanda but he never questioned the fact that she would not be faithful to him. Woody also admitted that he had slowed down in the bedroom but since he started taking the little blue pill, he thought the romance had been rekindled.

He also knew that "menopause" had caused some major changes in Amanda's personality. Not to mention, Woody had not been very sympathetic regarding her mood swings, hot flashes, and insomnia. But with all of that, there was no excuse for Amanda to commit adultery.

Now that Woody looked back on the last several months, there were signs that suggested that Amanda might have been having an affair—lateness from lunch dates, not telling her secretary about all her appointments, and going to work but not arriving until late in the afternoon.

Knowing all of this Woody never questioned his wife. The question was what did he want to do now? According to the letter, the affair was over. She never intended to leave him. The question was, did he want to end the marriage because she had gotten "some" on the side? That was what it was all about.

Regardless, Woody felt like a fool and he was hurt, angry and betrayed. He was relieved he had time to think before Amanda was due to come home from work. Woody knew if she had been there when he first made his discovery, he would have acted irrationally.

Over the years, Woody had thought about what he would do if he ever found out that Amanda cheated on him. The answer was always the same—he would divorce her. But that was when he was a younger man. Now he had grown old. Did he want to really start over? Is *"growing old"* a reason to stay with a woman who's been unfaithful? He had plenty of questions, but no answers.

When Woody thought about his situation, he could not help but think about the men from Sunday golf. This would have been an ideal topic for their after golf outing at Perkins. But how hilarious was that? Then again, he would have liked to have seen Lenny's face and heard what he had to say on the subject.

Ever since he and Amanda had the brunch, the men had not golfed on Sunday. The main reason was because of Russell being in the car accident. Everyone had been concerned about him. But this Sunday they had agreed to meet at Perkins to discuss the future of golfing on Sundays. As much as Woody would miss the guys, there was no way he was going to continue golfing with them.

CHAPTER 51

Raymond was curious as to why Donnie had not said anything to him about golfing on Sunday. Raymond had met these men and he saw nothing special about them. But for some reason Donnie liked them and he wanted to socialize with them. As far as Raymond was concerned, he did not care if he never saw them again in his life. Since Donnie did not seem as though he was going to bring up the subject of Sunday golf, Raymond did.

"Donnie, what are you going to do about golfing on Sunday?"

"I haven't made up my mind."

"Well, it seems to me that your little group might have dissolved ever since that Sunday brunch disaster. That was some Sunday afternoon. I know Amanda wished she had never had that bright idea."

"That's not why we have not been golfing on Sundays. We haven't been golfing because of Russell being in the automobile accident."

Raymond thought Donnie could be so naïve. In addition, he was not very observant.

Raymond responded, "Do you believe that? I'm telling you it's because of that Sunday brunch? When people have secrets they should know they're never secrets. Secrets are only secrets when you are the only one who knows what you don't want revealed."

"I agree but do you realize I still don't know everything that was going on that day. The only surprised developments I know about are Austin and Billy Ray being in interracial marriages and you and Vanessa. But there were times throughout the day when the tense facial expressions and whispers between husbands and wives could not go unnoticed. I have no idea what was causing all of that."

"Pleassse. You know enough."

"Well, I guess you're right. Not to mention the fact that I over heard somebody talking about something concerning Amanda and Lenny. Then I heard that Amanda knew Justin."

"Oh. I didn't hear all of that. Maybe when you meet Sunday with the other men they will come clean."

"Raymond, do you really think these men are going to share their dirty little secrets?"

"I think so. You want to know why?" Raymond did not expect an answer.

"Because the men already think, everyone knows their dirty little secrets have been exposed. So why not talk about them?"

"You might be right."

"Now, are you going to continue golfing on Sundays?"

Pausing for a minute, Donnie did not answer. He was not sure what he wanted to do. He would like to golf with the men but he was not sure he wanted that type of commitment—every Sunday. Raymond rolled his eyes and mumbled.

"It shouldn't be that hard of a decision."

"Raymond you are right but I just can't make up my mind." Donnie did not know why he was being so ambivalent about his decision.

"Maybe I'll golf some Sundays but not every Sunday. Then again, I might not have to make the decision. Maybe no one's going to golf. Anyway at this point, I have not made up my mind."

CHAPTER 52

"Suzanne, thank you so much for helping Russell. You are the greatest wife any man could ask for."
"What I did for Russell is what I do every day."
"I know it's your job but you helping Russell was very special to me."
"I know it was. I'm just glad I...we could help him. Don't give all the credit to me. You were a big help too."
"My part was so small but I did feel good helping him which brings me to a different subject that I want to discuss with you."
Justin took a moment while he thought about how he wanted to tell Suzanne about his career decision. He wanted to tell her sooner but he wanted to wait until he received his acceptance letter.
"What is it?"
"Well, what I've got to tell you..."
"What?" Suzanne could tell by the way Justin's eyes were twinkling that he was excited about whatever he had to tell her.
"I'm not going to golf on Sunday mornings."
"Justin, I told you before that..."
"Shhhh. I want and I need to be in church with you. Besides, I

made a major decision that I haven't shared with you yet. I hope you understand what I'm about to say."

Justin could not believe he had lost all of his exhilaration. He should not be worried because Suzanne is always supportive of whatever he decides to do. However, he realized now that he should have discussed this with her first. What had he been thinking about?

There was the baby and he would have to work part-time which meant reduced hours and income. Thinking about his career move now, Justin recognized that his plan was weak in certain areas. It had felt so right but now he had doubts. He had been sure God had led him to this decision. Beads of sweat had formed on his forehead.

Watching Justin, Suzanne was anxious. What could have caused him to go from a look of enthusiasm to a look of concern in a matter of minutes?

"Justin, please tell me what's going on."

Without thinking any more, he just blurted it out. "I applied to seminary school and I was accepted."

"What?" Teary eyed, Suzanne broke into a wide smile. She could hardly believe her ears.

"As you know I finished my college degree while I was in prison. However, even with a degree, I had a difficult time convincing someone to hire me as a counselor. But then I started thinking— every church should have a ministry program that could help prisoners when they first get released. The counseling I would provide would be to help bridge the gap from prison to the outside world."

Slowly he explained his plan and then gained momentum. "I want to focus my energy primarily on men but I would counsel women too. The counseling would involve resources, life-skills training, and life coping techniques. Hopefully, if we can get men to participate in the counseling, they will be less likely to be incarcerated again. I think I can give these men—hope, direction, and understanding. Mainly because I've been where they are coming from." Justin looked at Suzanne who was smiling like a Cheshire cat.

"I know in my heart that this is what God wants me to do.

Moreover, it can be an extension of the church's current prison ministry program."

Suzanne's eyes were full of joyful tears as she hugged her husband. At that moment, she could not have been any happier or prouder of her husband. Suzanne never gave up in praying for Justin and she knew God would answer her prayers. She only had to keep her faith. She knew God had a plan for Justin and he had finally put his life in God's hands.

CHAPTER 53

"Bob what are you going to do about golfing on Sunday?"

"I don't know yet. It depends on what the other men decide."

"Well you might want to think about how you spend your Sundays. You may not have the time to golf on Sundays."

"What are you talking about? Bob waited for an answer but Nessa did not reply right away.

"Basically, nothing has changed about Sundays. What's going on Nessa?"

Bob had no idea what was bothering his wife and she was not saying anything. She looked as if she was about to cry.

Tenderly, Bob said, "Nessa, it can't be that bad. What's wrong?"

"Bob I don't know where to begin." Nessa was concerned about what she had to tell her husband.

"Just tell me. You're beginning to worry me."

"I should have told you this several weeks ago after I had my doctor's appointment."

Nessa's tone had turned more serious than he had ever heard her. Bob was uneasy as he questioned her.

"What's wrong? Are you sick?" Swallowing hard, she looked at him and smiled slightly.

"No nothing like that. I want you to know that I never expected that something like this would happen at my age."

"Nessa you're scaring me. If it's menopause, we'll deal with it." Nervously, she shook her head no.

"Please Nessa, just tell me what's going on?"

"I'm trying. It's just so hard to say."

Walking over to her, Bob hugged her. He cuddled her against his chest until he heard Nessa say.

"We're going to have a baby."

"What? You said…" Bob looked at his wife with wide eyes.

"I know what I said. With the missed periods and the God awful mood swings I just assumed I might have been at the beginning stages of menopause."

"But Nessa, we haven't used protection, so you should have thought maybe you might get pregnant."

"No. I didn't think about pregnancy because the doctor clearly told me that my chances of getting pregnant were slim to none. So I thought I could not get pregnant…you know because of what he said and my age."

"Well, it goes to show you, the doctor was wrong."

Bob showered her with kisses until she could barely breathe. Stopping he looked at his wife who was crying.

"I love you. I hope those are tears of joy."

Laughing pensively, Vanessa said, "Do you know how old I'll be when our baby graduates from high school?"

Making a scrunched face, Bob said, "Who cares? I won't be that far behind you. Besides if you keep aging the way you're doing, everyone will think I married a younger woman."

"You make me feel so good. Now, what about Sunday golf?"

"It depends on the other men."

Vanessa said, "Well, the way I see it I think that the Sunday brunch might have derailed your Sunday golf."

"Why do you say that?"

"Well, it seems that some of you men had secrets that they had not shared and were not willing to tell."

"Like what?"

"Well, you didn't tell any of the men about my age."

"That wasn't a big deal. Besides, it never came up. What else?"

"Well...the brothers-in-law. Then there was something going on with Amanda and that Lenny guy..." Vanessa's voice trailed off.

"We must have been at a different brunch. I mean everyone was surprised about Austin and Billy Ray being brothers-in-law but no one really cares." Vanessa went back to figuring out who would be golfing.

"Well, let's see. We know Russell probably won't be golfing. What about Donnie?"

"Why wouldn't he continue golfing?"

"Okay. He's in. What about Justin?"

"Hard to tell."

"What about Woody?"

"Maybe. Listen Nessa wait until I meet with the guys. Again, you must have picked up a vibe or something that I missed at the brunch. The only one that will probably have a problem and won't be able to golf is Russell because of the car accident."

Bob could see the wheels rolling in Nessa's head. Yes, she was pregnant and he was happy but there was no reason why he could not golf on Sunday.

CHAPTER 54

"Ebony, it was thoughtful of you to invite Austin, Jessica, Eloise, and Lenny over to play cards."

"Well, I always say you can tell a lot about a person if and when they play cards."

"Like what?"

"Well, Hand and Foot is a card game that is so easy to play that I can tell you if a person is able to socialize, talk, concentrate, and yet be competitive."

"So, what did you think about me when we first played cards?"

Teasingly, she rolled her eyes and said, "That you didn't know a thing about playing cards."

"Oh really. If my memory serves me right, I beat you at every card game we played."

"Yeah, because you cheated."

"No, I didn't." The doorbell saved Ebony and Billy Ray from any additional discussion about playing cards.

"Welcome. Come in."

Ebony yelled, Billy Ray, everyone's here."

Hugs and kisses were exchanged. Lenny did not participate. His family was not big on giving hugs and kisses but Austin's family always seemed to greet one another with genuine affection.

Eloise said, "I couldn't believe the timing. Just as we got out of our car, Austin and Jessica were parking their car."

"Ebony, would you please get your baby sister something cold to drink?"

"Excuse me Eloise, you know where the kitchen is."

Eloise whined, "But I'm a guest, remember."

"Since when?" Eloise stomped off to the kitchen to get a cola when she thought about Lenny.

"Lenny do you want something to drink?"

"Not right now, but thanks," he answered.

Billy Ray said, "As you all can see Ebony and I have already set up everything for our card game."

Then Billy Ray asked, Lenny, do you know how to play Hand and Foot?"

"A little. Eloise's been teaching me."

"That's good. The game is so easy that we can always help you as we play."

Before the men noticed, the women had gone to the kitchen and were whispering. It was Austin who stated that they were probably gossiping. Just as he had made the statement, the three women walked in.

"Excuse me dear husband. What were you saying about us gossiping?" asked Jessica.

"Nothing. I just said you all were probably talking about something you didn't want us to hear." Austin tried to cover up what he had really said.

Austin asked, "Well, what were you all talking about?"

Jessica answered, "We were wondering if you all were going to continue golfing on Sunday?"

Lenny looked at Billy Ray and then to Austin. They were noncommittal and didn't answer Jessica.

Finally Lenny answered, "I can't speak for the other men but I still want to golf on Sundays. We were all making such good progress. It will be a shame if we have to stop."

"Yeah, we were making some progress. But I don't think Russell will probably be able to golf considering his wife's condition." Billy Ray commented.

"You're probably right Billy Ray. I noticed you and Austin didn't say whether you're going to golf?"

Billy Ray glanced at Ebony and she mouthed—it's up to you. Austin looked at Jessica who shrugged her shoulders.

Billy Ray said, "I think I'll wait and see who's going to continue golfing on Sundays."

Austin agreed with Billy Ray and said, "Let's see if anyone besides you Lenny wants to continue golfing on Sundays. If the men are going to continue, we're in if the men aren't then maybe we can think of another way so that the three of us can golf. As we improve, maybe the women would want to join us."

"Yeah, that might work." Lenny smiled at Eloise.

"Okay guys with that settled, let's play Hand and Foot. The women decided that we can have more fun if we play women against men." Ebony smiled broadly.

Billy Ray jumped at the challenge. "I don't believe you women want to take us on. How about a little wager?"

Jessica looked at Ebony and then at Eloise. They gave her the thumbs up.

Jessica asked, "What do you have in mind fellows?"

"Losers clean the kitchen and that means loading and unloading the dishwasher and washing, drying, and putting away the pots after dinner for a week."

The women huddled and conferred. After several minutes the women agreed to the wager.

Lenny commented, "Eloise, we'll have to decide on something else for our wager." Mischievously, he smiled.

Teasing Austin said, "Let's get started and teach these ladies how to play cards."

CHAPTER 55

As far as Lenny knew everyone would be at Perkins for breakfast. No one had called to say otherwise. Lenny was the first to arrive so he thought. When Lenny pulled his car into a parking space, he noticed Woody sitting in his car. He wondered why he had not gone inside the restaurant.

The minute Woody saw Lenny pulling his car into a parked space, he opened his car door. Getting out of his car, Woody moved quickly toward Lenny's car. As Lenny opened and closed his car door, Woody was beside it. However, Lenny did not notice that Woody was standing there.

"Good morn…"

Before Lenny could finish his greeting he felt Woody's full fist connect with his nose.

"That's for fucking my wife."

Lenny let out a yell. As he reached for his nose, another blow hit Lenny's mid-section.

He doubled over and groaned, "What the hell."

There was no mistake Woody had just informed Lenny that he knew about the affair. Quickly, Woody turned and started walking in the direction of his car. Stopping, he turned back around.

"Oh, and by the way, you can take your Sunday golf and stick it up your ass." Woody took a few steps back to where Lenny was standing. He did not want to shout.

"If I have not made myself clear, it means I won't be golfing on Sundays. Please tell the guys I said hello. My decision has nothing to do with them."

Turning back around, he headed to his car. Getting in his car, he did not hesitate as he sped off.

Taking a handkerchief from his pocket, Lenny put it to his nose. Blood was flowing from his nose like a running faucet. Lenny leaned his head back in hopes that it would stop bleeding.

Managing to walk inside Perkins without too much blood falling from his nose, Lenny rushed straight to the men's room. Taking paper from the toilet paper roll, Lenny stuffed his nose with the tissue. His nose was still bleeding but not profusely as it had when Woody first hit him.

Before going out to the restaurant, Lenny tried to wipe some of the blood off his polo shirt. He was thankful that his shirt was multicolored. The blood was blending into the red, blue, and brown design.

Lenny was still a little shaken. He could not believe Woody hit him but he could understand it. He guessed he deserved it. He knew how he would have reacted if he had discovered that his wife had cheated on him. Lenny was an easier target than Mandy...Amanda.

By the time Lenny left the men's room, his bleeding nose had just about stopped. Entering the dining area, he saw that all the men had arrived and were already seated. Lenny was glad they had not witnessed Woody hitting him. Approaching the table, Lenny held up his hand to silence the inquiring remarks.

"Hello everyone. The short story is that Woody sucker punched me in the parking lot. The punch was for screwing his wife. You all don't need to know all the sordid details but I will say I didn't know that his wife was the woman I was having an affair with. I knew the woman was married but not to Woody." The stunned looks on the men's faces were of disbelief.

Russell asked, "How did he find out?"

"I don't know and he didn't say and I didn't ask." Lenny paused for a minute and was sorry he had snapped at Russell. Adjusting the tissue that was trying to slip out his nose, he continued.

"Woody did say to tell you all hello and that he would not be golfing on Sundays. It had nothing to do with any of you."

"Well that's rather obvious," sarcastically, Billy Ray said and continued.

"Since that secret is out, do we need to see what other secrets might keep us from golfing on Sundays?" Looking directly at Donnie when he finished.

"Why are you looking at me? I don't have anything to hide. You all know I'm gay."

Austin smiled and added, "Well Billy Ray and I saw you and Stuart at the far end of the parking lot. You two looked pretty cozy."

"Whoa. I think you misunderstood what..." Donnie tried to provide an explanation for what Billy Ray and Austin thought they saw.

Billy Ray cut him off. "It's okay. I mean that's your business."

"Well gentlemen can we agree that what went on in the parking lot, stays in the parking lot?" Donnie looked at Billy Ray and Austin. They smiled and gave him the thumbs up.

CHAPTER 56

"Well, do we continue to golf on Sundays or not?" Bob wanted to know. Rather than answering Bob, Lenny made a suggestion.

"Why don't we place our breakfast orders then discuss golfing on Sunday." It was unanimous, they would order their food first and then talk. The orders were placed and Russell went first.

"You all know that Connie and I were in a car accident. Fortunately, we did not receive any injuries that were life threatening. While Connie was recuperating in the hospital from her multiple injuries, I made the decision to divorce her." When Russell stopped, all he could hear were outbursts for support of his decision.

"For the first time in a long time, I feel like I'm in control of my life. With me being a single parent, I need to spend my Sundays with my children. Another thing you all don't know is that I have Justin to thank for helping me make my decision regarding Connie."

All eyes went to Justin. Justin threw up his hands. "Hey it wasn't me. It was my beautiful, pregnant wife Suzanne." Everyone congratulated Justin on his upcoming baby.

"Well Justin with the baby coming I guess you won't be golfing on Sundays," commented Donnie.

"Well, you're partially right. I will be spending my Sundays with Suzanne but mostly I'll be spending my Sundays in church. I've been accepted into seminary school to become a minister. What I never told you all is that I spent three years in prison."

Justin waited for the reactions. No one said anything but Justin did notice widened eyes of surprise when he mentioned he had served time in prison.

"When I become a minister, it is my hope to provide counseling for men being released from prison, especially those that are first time offenders and those that have not committed violent crimes."

As an after thought Justin added, "Women are included but my main focus is on men." Justin waited to see if anyone had a question.

"This program will be an extension of my church's current prison ministry program. I will be helping these men and women to adjust to life outside of prison, which isn't easy to do."

As Justin explained to the men what he intended to do for ex-cons, the men applauded Justin for his efforts. They also thanked him for trusting them enough to share about being in prison. Justin was overwhelmed with gratitude regarding all the men's positive and supportive comments.

"Justin, let us know if and when you have to preach a trial sermon. I know we will all be there." Russell spoke for everyone as the men nodded in agreement.

"Thanks guys that means a lot to me. I plan on keeping in touch and I will definitely let you know how I'm doing."

Donnie shared, "Justin, I don't know if you know it but your program might qualify for some of that government grant money that is available for faith-based ministry programs. Call me and I will give you the information that I have. In addition, I will be more than happy to help you write the grant proposal."

"Oh man. Thanks. I don't know what to say."

Donnie said, "It's okay. Thanks will do."

"I don't mean to change subjects but Justin and Suzanne aren't the only couple having a baby. Nessa is pregnant."

Bob's face said it all. His eyes were twinkling and he was smiling from ear to ear. Everyone congratulated Bob. They wished him the best.

Donnie said, "Hey Bob, you and Justin can do baby things together or whatever they do now days. If nothing else, you can always call on Russell. He's already a seasoned parent."

"We'll need all the help we can get. Maybe Suzanne can talk to Nessa. The only thing is that my wife is a little older than me and she's sensitive about it."

Suddenly Bob stopped. It never occurred to Bob that he might have something to worry about.

"Nessa is 38 years old so I'm hoping that the pregnancy won't cause any problems for her and the baby." Seeing the concerned look on Bob's face, Donnie said as a comfort.

"Man, you need to watch television a little more or you wouldn't be too concerned about your wife's age. Recently, it was reported on the news that there was a woman in her 60's who just gave birth to a healthy baby. So if this 60-year old woman can have a baby, I know as healthy as Vanessa looks she won't have any problems. Besides modern medicine is amazing."

Smiling Bob felt relieved. He was not aware that women were having babies so old. He appreciated Donnie sharing that with him.

"Oh and I'm willing to golf on Sundays if anyone else is."

"Billy Ray and I will golf too."

"Okay, let's see, so far we have Bob, Billy Ray, Austin, and me. What about you Donnie?"

"Well, I can't golf every Sunday but I can golf as a substitute if one of you guys can't golf. Is that okay?"

"I guess you'll be getting private lessons." Billy Ray let out a laugh.

"No. I will not be getting private lessons. I'm not going to discuss this with you guys." Donnie said, trying to hide his embarrassment.

"Donnie if you want to golf as a substitute, I'll call you when one of us are not going to be able to golf."

"You got it." To be truthful Donnie wanted to golf but he knew Raymond was not trilled with him golfing on Sundays with these men. If Donnie did not know better, he would think that Raymond was jealous. What Raymond does not know is that he might have a reason to be jealous but not because of his golfing on Sundays.

"Bob does your wife golf?"

"Yes why?" Lenny smiled. He had an idea.

"Why don't we form a new Sunday golf group?" The men wanted to know with whom? They were not keen on the idea of finding some new men to join them.

"Your wives and my future wife." Lenny could not believe that came out of his mouth. Timidly, he looked at Austin. Taken back, Austin laughed and teased.

"You're not serious about marrying my baby sister?"

"Yes I am. I really love your sister and will always be grateful for you introducing me to her. Keep in mind I haven't proposed to her yet so please don't mention this to Jessica or Ebony. Besides she might say no."

"I don't know what to say. I know you two have been seeing each other on a pretty regular basis but I had no idea your relationship had reached this level." Billy Ray added and said.

"I know Ebony doesn't know. In fact she just talked to Eloise yesterday. But then again, Eloise is usually tight lipped about her personal life. I do know Eloise has really softened and she seems much happier. I guess we owe the change to you Lenny." Billy Ray let out a chuckle.

"I still can't get over it. I tell you something else. I bet there's no one else in our family who would guess that you want to marry Eloise."

Looking concerned Lenny had doubts for the first time about Eloise saying *"yes"* to his proposal. It never occurred to him that she might not want to get married. Marriage was his idea. Lenny loved Eloise and wanted to spend the rest of his life with her. Now he just needed to ask her.

"I think it's great you want to marry Eloise and it will be great to have another man in the family. However, whatever you do, please talk to her old man—sorry Austin. I mean you better talk to Mr.

Hayes before you ask Eloise. He's old fashioned like that." Billy Ray offered as advice.

"You got my vote of approval but Billy Ray is right. You need to talk to my dad about marrying Eloise but I can guarantee you, he'll be more than delighted for you to marry that woman."

Through the laughter Lenny thanked Austin and Billy Ray. He would definitely take their advise about talking to Mr. Hayes before asking Eloise to marry him. He wanted their relationship to start off on the right foot.

"Now, can we get back to the business at hand—golfing?"

Billy Ray got on Lenny because he was the one who got them off track. Lenny agreed, but he was so excited about his decision to marry Eloise that he wanted to tell them. The men discussed back and forth alternatives regarding Sunday golf.

They had just finished eating their food as they ended their discussion about golfing on Sunday. Lenny had suggested that they golf with the women. Not all the guys were happy about changing up with their current arrangements.

"Come on guys, it will be fun. Actually, we're not really golfing with the women. We're just including them into our Sunday golf." From the looks on everyone's face, they still were not convinced but listened as Lenny explained.

"Look, it's quite simple. I'll arrange for two sets of tee times, just like I do now. The women will make up the first foursome. The men will make up the second foursome. We'll be golfing together but separately. As usual, we'll have our outing at Perkins but the women will sit at one table and the men will sit at another table."

When Lenny finished he let the men ponder over how golfing on Sundays with their wives and significant others would work. There was silence and no one said anything.

Finally, Austin broke the silence and said, "Lenny, I think you are really clever. For one, you have just made our wives and significant others happy by including them, and two, you found a way so that we can continue our Sunday golf."

Printed in the United States
66234LVS00002B/172-189